BRAYDON'S BRIDE

SEVEN BRIDES FOR SEVEN BROTHERS
BOOK THREE

KATHLEEN LAWLESS

ISBN ebook: 978-0-9937701-9-7

ISBN print: 978-1-989873-51-9

Seven Brides for Seven Brothers Reviews

What reviewers are saying about the *Seven Brides for Seven Brothers* series...

"GREAT SERIES!!!" Top 500 reviewer

"If you have not picked up the series, do yourself a favor, you will be glad you do."

"I loved the continuity in the series—and the resolution"

"Sweet and romantic."

"This entire series is going into my library to be read again and again."

"I just love reading Kathleen's books—they keep me coming back for more."

If you haven't already done so, sign up for my VIP Reader's Newsletter and be the first to hear about free books, fan-priced sales, and my new series. Details at the end of the book.

Dedication

Dedicated to John, my love.

And Shelley, proofreader extraordinaire.

CHAPTER 1

The Arizona sun shone brightly overhead, raining its golden sheen on the church bell tower, which peeled happy news throughout the entire town of Bullet. The church bells faded away, to be replaced by the familiar notes of the bridal march inside the small church.

To Henrietta, it appeared the entire town was on hand to witness the marriage between their beloved pianist and one of the seven Mason brothers. As this was the second Mason wedding in a short amount of time, there were more than a few murmured speculations as to which brother would be next to get hitched.

Seated next to Sir Percy in the second row of pews, Henrietta stirred restlessly, unable to tear her gaze from the dark and handsome Braydon Mason. She didn't want her gaze drawn that way. Had no intention of being distracted from the adventure that had brought her to Arizona in the first place. Still, something about him stirred feelings she had long thought lost forever.

As the happy newlyweds paraded down the center aisle,

Percy stood and offered her his arm. "Nothing like a Valentine's Day wedding to bring out the romantic in us all."

Henrietta slanted him a glance. "You, Percy? Romantic? Seriously?"

Percy smoothed the cuff of his formal jacket. "Life isn't only about adventure and hunting treasure, my dear."

"It is for me," Henrietta said as they, along with the other wedding guests, shuffled their way out of the church and onto the tidy main street of Bullet. Their way was slow going as the many guests stopped to congratulate the bride and groom and greet the rest of the wedding party.

Percy turned to her. "Dear, Henny. One day I'll remind you what you said here today."

"Don't be holding your breath," she said.

Percy, ever the social butterfly, was soon off gladhanding the locals, leaving Henrietta to hover off to the side, the way she preferred.

"You clean up good."

Henrietta whirled, recognizing the arrogant drawl of Braydon Mason, looming over her in his usual irritating fashion.

"Who even knew you owned a dress?"

She jutted out her chin. "And who knew you owned a suit?" Truth was, Braydon had the type of build clothes love. Broad shoulders filled out his jacket, which draped perfectly across his lean abdomen and brushed muscular thighs encased in formal trousers. A crisp white shirt emphasized the sun-burnished tone of his skin and made his dark hair appear even darker in contrast.

"Bought it for Brody's wedding last year," Braydon said cheerfully. "Expect to get plenty more wear out of it if any of the other brothers fall into the marital trap."

Henrietta sniffed, not bothering to mention she considered marriage as much of a trap as he did. One she had narrowly escaped in her native country of Argentina.

As the wedding party started in the direction of Georgina's Café for the post-nuptial celebration, she heard Braydon being hailed by one of his brothers.

"I'll see you over there," Braydon said.

"Not if I see you first," Henrietta said, under her breath. The problem was, Bullet was small, and avoiding someone was nearly impossible. Thank goodness she had the dig site to go hide out.

"Were you being wooed by one of the handsome Mason brothers?" Percy asked, as he rejoined her.

"Insulted is more like it."

Percy laughed his dry, British laugh. "Oh, my goodness. That must mean he likes you more than just a little, my dear." A statement Henrietta didn't dignify with a response as she followed him to the town's only eatery.

"It is certainly a good thing Georgina expanded her business last year," Percy said as they claimed seats at an empty table inside the newly refurbished café.

"Yes," Henrietta said. "It's nice to see a spinster do well in the world of business."

"I'd be careful who you go calling 'spinster'. I dare say Georgina is not much older than you are."

Henrietta gave him a brilliant smile. "I'm not a spinster. I'm a world-travelling treasure-hunter. There's a difference. Spinsters secretly long to get married."

But she had noticed lately the way Georgina had started taking extra care with her appearance. A change of hairstyle and some stylish new clothing had literally stripped years from the other woman, whose energy seemed positively youthful as she raced about the café seeing to the last-minute details of the wedding feast.

Percy pushed back his chair. "Come my dear, the reception line is up. Time to go pay our respects to the happy couple."

Western weddings were certainly nothing like those at home, Henrietta mused as they moved through the receiving line. She hadn't been in Bullet for long, but she was amazed at how many people she recognized.

She stopped in front of Laura Mason, matron of honor, who had recently wed Brody Mason, the head of the Mason brother's clan. Other than one set of twins, none of the men were actual blood brothers, yet they appeared closer than Henrietta's own nine brothers, who seemed to always be in a row over one thing or another.

"You look lovely, Laura."

Laura's skin flushed a becoming shade of pink as she rested one hand on the barely visible bump at her waistline. "It's a relief to know I should manage the day without running off to be sick."

Henrietta repressed a shudder. Did all women look so happy when they were expecting? As the youngest in her family, she had little experience in the matter and no desire to educate herself.

The Argentine government encouraged its people to have large families, a fate she had barely escaped when she left Argentina for England, where she attended Oxford University. Her family claimed her education effectively killed any hope of suitors and had basically disowned her.

"You look beautiful as well," Laura said. "I know those britches you wear for your treasure quest are more practical, but it's nice to see you in a dress."

"I have no plans to make it a habit." Henrietta gave Laura a quick hug and moved on to shake hands with the groom's best man, Laura's husband Brody.

His face creased in a huge smile when he saw her. He pulled her against him in a giant bear hug. "I'll never be able to thank you enough for your part in helping rescue Laura."

"I was happy to be able to help."

"Still. I would have loved to see a tiny thing like you take on that lumbering buffoon and set him on his ear."

"I learned early on, a woman needs to be able to defend herself," Henrietta said.

"And I bet you've had lots of practice." Braydon stood next to Brody, shamelessly eavesdropping on their conversation.

"Bray." Brody's voice was low and warning. "Mind your manners around Miss Henrietta."

"I only meant a woman as beautiful as Henny must be fighting off suitors on a daily basis," Braydon said.

Henrietta gave him a look designed to freeze water. "Somehow, I doubt that's what you meant, Mr. Mason."

"Braydon," he said smoothly. "Too many Mr. Masons here under one roof."

At least one too many, Henrietta thought, as she relayed her best wishes to the happy couple, Bradley and Amanda, and thanked them for inviting her.

"Sleepy little Bullet hasn't been the same since you and Sir Percy arrived," Amanda told her. "In a good way."

"It's been a godsend being able to rent your family home as our headquarters," Henrietta said.

Amanda beamed. "Stay as long as you like."

Henrietta refrained from mentioning she seldom stayed very long in any one place and preferred it that way.

"I told you Braydon likes you," Percy said gleefully as they made their way toward the buffet table.

"Percy, your life barely exists outside of your reference books. You know nothing of human nature."

"I've learned a bit hanging out with you, Hen."

Henrietta gave her dear friend a quick, appreciative pat on the back as they picked up empty plates and joined the line of guests awaiting their turn at the food table. The babble in the room was immediately silenced by a sharp clink of silverware against glass. Henrietta shook her head and bit back a smile. "Poor Amanda."

Percy cocked her a glance before he turned his attention to where the bride and groom were exchanging a lustful kiss to the noisy whistles of approval from their wedding guests. "She doesn't look like a woman in need of pity. I'd say she looks a darn sight happier than you lately."

Henrietta speared a slice of ham and placed it on her plate. "I'll be dancing for joy once we find that buried ship of pearls."

"I prefer the lead-up to the discovery, myself," Percy said. "It's like one giant puzzle. Once the pieces all come together, I tend to lose interest."

"Yes, but our benefactors don't. They count on our successes."

"It does provide them great cocktail party chit-chat," Percy said. "Luckily, there is always another treasure to chase and someone willing to fund the adventure."

"Arm chair travelers," Henrietta said with disdain. "Ones who love to recount the story as if they were there in person."

"And they pay dearly for that privilege. Not everyone is cut out to make the trek to Egypt and parts beyond."

"Who was in Egypt?" Braydon interrupted. Henrietta whirled, angry he was once again eavesdropping on a private conversation, but Percy continued to be ever the diplomat.

"Henny and I were there last year, old boy. Damned hot."

Braydon followed them toward their table. "What were you after?"

"Hoping to find one of the pharaoh's tombs. No such luck, though. Ever since the Egyptians stopped building pyramids because they were getting looted, later rulers were laid to rest in huge caves dug into the hillsides. Many of them are still unaccounted for." He sighed. "Unfortunately, that fact has also encouraged every so-called treasure hunter who hopes to find his fortune."

Braydon gave Henrietta a slow, assessing look, starting with her toes and moving slowly, lingering on her breasts and face. "Doesn't sound like much of a place for a woman."

Henrietta hated the fact that her skin prickled from the power radiated by his perusal, almost as if she'd spent too much time lately in the sun. Suddenly she was uncomfortably warm. A trickle of dampness ran between her breasts. Breasts which felt unaccountably heavy and achy.

She took her seat with a jolt and glared up at Braydon for ruining what had started out to be a most pleasant day. "Aren't you needed at the head table? Giving a toast or something?"

He smiled down at her as if he knew exactly why she was trying to get rid of him. And was enjoying the way his presence unsettled her. "We'll have to chat again soon. I'd love to hear more about your adventures."

Percy, chimed in. "Anytime. You know where to find us, old chap."

Henrietta heaved a sigh of relief as Braydon sauntered back toward the bride and groom. "Don't encourage him," she hissed under her breath.

Percy shook his elegant head. "Darling Henny. Men like Braydon Mason don't need encouragement. They thrive on any sort of challenge."

Henrietta sniffed. "As long as he doesn't consider me one. Laura warned me he fancies himself quite the ladies' man. He was raised in a brothel, of all places."

Percy laughed out loud, causing a few of the guests to look their way, wondering if they had missed a good joke. "I'm not sure if I ought to envy the bloke or pity him."

Just then Georgina, the café owner, stopped at their table. "Enjoying everything?"

"You've done a wonderful job," Henrietta said. "It's so refreshing to see a woman being successful in business."

"This is my first wedding here," Georgina confessed. "I couldn't have managed anything like this without Miss Laura's help."

Henrietta frowned. "I wouldn't think, in her condition, Laura would be much help in a café."

"It's because of her I was able to manage the expansion." Georgina clapped a hand to her mouth the second the words popped out. "Please don't tell her I told you that. I don't think she wants folks to know."

"Your secret is safe," Percy assured her. As Georgina bustled off, other wedding guests carrying plates of food joined their table. The conversation turned from serious to lively as the gentlemen indulged freely in the kegs of beer being offered.

Next thing Henrietta knew, a glass of Champagne appeared at her elbow and all eyes were on the head table, which meant she had to work extra hard not to look at Braydon.

No easy feat when he was the one presenting the toast to the bride. Red-headed Amanda blushed becomingly at the charming things he said about her, before he finished up by wishing her and Bradley a lifetime of happiness.

"Please join me in a toast to the bride," Braydon said.

Along with the other guests, Henrietta dutifully raised her glass, then downed her Champagne in a single swallow.

Percy gave her an admiring look. "One of the things I've always admired about you, Hen, is your ability to hold your liquor."

"That's what comes from being raised on a winery. From a very early age we drank wine as if it was water. And learned to tell a good vintage from a bad one."

Braydon took his seat, relieved his part in the day's proceedings was finally over. Public speaking was not exactly something he enjoyed, and the fact that he was among friends didn't make it any easier to have all eyes upon him.

What he didn't object to was having Henrietta's intelligent green eyes directed his way. Hard to say what intrigued him most about her. Maybe the fact that she wasn't like any women he had ever known, and his world had consisted primarily of women for as long as he could remember. Henny, with her striking Latin beauty, unconventional mode of dress, snapping emerald eyes, and sharp tongue, was an irresistible combination.

Blake, on his left, leaned over toward him. "Good job, Bray. Glad it didn't fall to me," he added, watching Braydon fold up his scrawled-on notepaper and tuck it into his pocket.

Braydon nodded. Blake was smart as a whip, especially with anything mechanical. It was just a shame that letters and numbers made no sense to him. Braydon, who had learned to read at a young age, couldn't imagine not being able to learn about the world through books.

He gave Blake's arm a companionable squeeze. "How about we agree you say the toast at my wedding? Since I'm never getting married, you've got nothing to worry about."

Blake's smile brightened his day. Generally speaking, the Masons all got along and respected the unique skills each of them brought to the ranch. Still, it couldn't be easy knowing you were different from all the others when it came to reading and writing.

"Are Percy and Miss Henrietta getting any closer to finding that sunken ship?" Blake asked.

"Hard to say," Braydon said. "Sounds to me like a total wild goose chase. But I did wangle an invitation to go out and see where they're working."

Blake gave him a knowing look. "Why do I get the feeling it's more about the lady and less about what she's up to while she's here?"

Braydon punched him gently on the closest arm. "She's hardly my type."

Blake laughed. "They're all your type. Henrietta, though, might be a bit more challenging than most. I hear she's traveled to lots of faraway places."

"So she claims. Which begs the question, what's she doing here in boring old Bullet?"

"Why don't you go ask her to dance?" Blake said. "Looks like Percy's abandoned her."

Braydon glanced in Henrietta's direction. Sure enough, she was sitting there alone. She hadn't been in town long enough to make a lot of friends. And from what he could tell, she wouldn't have much in common with the women-folk of Bullet.

"You're right." He pushed to his feet. "It's time someone took pity on the poor thing."

Blake's laugh came out more like a snort. "Why do I get the feeling she won't much cotton to your pitying nature?"

"Because, my friend, you know diddly about women."

HENRIETTA WATCHED Braydon rise and saunter her way, making her feel like something akin to an animal in a trap. She rose to her feet before he reached her, scanning the room for the nearest exit, but only made it two steps before he caught her arm. She glanced back, horrified to see he held her shawl and her reticule in one large, sun-browned hand.

"Forgetting something?"

There was no mistaking the teasing glint in his dark eyes. She tossed her head proudly. "Not at all. I was just..." She glanced around looking for an excuse for her attempt to flee. "I was just going for another glass of Champagne."

"Great idea. I could use a beer myself." Before she knew it, her hand was tucked in the crook of his arm and secured there with his free hand. She could feel the warmth of his clasp send tingles of awareness up her arm and beyond.

Henrietta felt the curious gaze from more than a few pairs of eyes following their progress, and much as she wanted to pull away and tell Braydon Mason to keep his filthy hands to himself, she reminded herself there was a time and a place for everything. She was the newcomer here, and hence more closely watched than those who had lived here their entire lives. She also knew she was something of a curiosity to the locals.

"'Nother beer, Bray?" the bartender greeted them.

"And Champagne for the lady, Mitch."

"Thank you," she said, accepting the glass of Champagne Braydon held her way, relieved when he released her to pick up their drinks from the bar.

"My pleasure." The way he watched her over the rim of his glass implied his pleasures were vast and varied. And that he wasn't above sharing.

Two could play at that game!

She leaned against the bar, not taking her eyes from him. "I hear the women in town are all wondering who will be the next Mason brother down the aisle, and with which lucky lady."

"I've got four other brothers in the running. I'll sit that race out."

"Don't be saying that too loudly," Henrietta said. "I can't bear the sight of female tears."

"One more thing we have in common."

"I wasn't aware we had anything in common, Mr. Mason."

"I told you. Braydon." He reached forward and tucked a loose strand of hair behind her ear with an easy familiarity that annoyed her. She went to bat his hand away, but he caught her hand in his and raised it to his mouth. Before she could jerk free, his tongue made the most delicious hot swirls across her palm, at the same time his thumb stroked the sensitive underside of her wrist.

Pulling her hand away was the furthest thing from her mind.

Instead, she dashed her glass of Champagne in his face.

CHAPTER 2

The sun was setting, leaving the western skyline a
wash of orange and pink streaks above the horizon by
the time the wedding celebrations wrapped up and the
Masons piled into the buckboard wagon to head home.

Goodbyes were exchanged as the bride and groom left in
the opposite direction from the Copper Moon ranch to
spend two nights in Yuma. Braydon saw Laura, his sister-in-
law, try to cover a yawn.

"Better get your wife home, Brody, before she falls asleep
on us."

Brody, who was driving the team cast an affectionate
glance in Laura's direction. "I wanted to leave earlier. She
wouldn't have it."

"I was having a good time dancing," Laura said. "Pretty
soon, I'll be too fat to move."

"I doubt that, love," Brody said.

Laura turned her attentions Braydon's way. "What
happened between you and Henrietta?" she asked.

The twins guffawed, and elbowed each other. "Musta
said something she didn't cotton to. Isn't that right?"

"Lay off," Blake said to the twins, and Braydon inwardly winced. Blake meant well, but Braydon didn't need anyone leaping to his defense.

"I always thought Braydon had a way with the ladies," Benjamin drawled from where he sat slouched in the back of the wagon. "Guess I was mistaken."

"Or Miss Henrietta isn't much of a lady," one of the twins said.

"Seeing as how she stomps around in those men's trousers all the time," the other twin said.

"Those are not men's trousers," Laura said sharply. "They are very practical for the work she does."

Both twins looked sulky at being reprimanded. "Never met no gal who liked sleeping in a tent and digging around in the mud all day."

"Really?" Brody said. "Not even when you two were on the road conning unsuspecting folks out of their hard-earned wages?"

The twins squirmed uncomfortably. No one liked finding himself on Brody's bad side. And now that Brody and Laura were married, having the two of them look askance your way was more than most of the brothers could handle.

They all loved Laura, and went out of their way to ensure her safety, especially after she'd been attacked by that human garbage Hawkes.

Speaking of Hawkes, they were driving past his spread right now. Braydon wondered if it was instinct that had Brody speed up the horses. He placed his hand on his holstered gun and saw the other men did as well. None of them was about to be taking any chances. Especially with precious cargo like Laura Mason on board.

"Looked like Hawkes was about the only one in town not invited to the wedding," Blake said.

"Him and the sheriff," Benjamin said.

Braydon nodded to himself. It was a well-known fact those two were in cahoots. And not on the right side of the law.

They passed Hawkes's spread without incident and had almost reached the ranch when Braydon saw a shadowy figure staggering in the middle of the road as if lost.

"Watch out!" he called to Brody.

"Whoa!" The buckboard shuddered as Brody pulled up the team of horses. "Sir Percy? What in the blazes man? What are you doing out here in the pitch black? Nearabouts ran you over."

Braydon and the twins wasted no time vaulting over the side of the wagon. As they approached Percy, they saw he had a handkerchief pressed against his forehead.

"Damn horse thieves," Percy spat out. "Didn't see them until it was too late."

Braydon grabbed his arm. "Were you alone?"

Percy gave his head a sorrowful shake. "Henny got off a shot. Made them angry, I guess, because they grabbed her up and took her with them."

Braydon felt his gut clench. "How many were there?"

"Four, from what I could tell," Percy said. "There could have been others hanging back. I tried to stop them and got a rifle barrel in my face for my trouble."

"Would you menfolk kindly quit your jabbering and get Sir Percy into the wagon so we can take him to the house and see just how badly he's hurt?" Laura said.

When Laura issued orders, they were obeyed to a man. In minutes, the group was under way and arrived at the ranch in record time.

15

Braydon saw Brody try to convince Laura to head to the nearby cabin he'd built for the two of them after they were married, but Laura wasn't having it. She marched ahead into the main ranch house, issuing orders.

"One of you boys stoke up the fire. We'll be needing hot water. The rest of you, get some lanterns lit. A body can barely see their hand in front of their face. Bishop, you go fetch the first aid kit. Sir Percy, let's go get you settled over here by the fire. Where in Sam Hill is that lantern?"

Brody brought a lit lantern close while the others scurried off like ants on an ant hill. Braydon hung back to talk to Percy. "Anyone you recognized?"

Percy shook his head. "Afraid not. Hats pulled low."

"Where in the blazes were you and Henny going so late? Why didn't you stay in town?"

"I wanted to, but Hen was impatient to get back to the dig site in order to get an early start in the morning."

"Not a lick of sense, either of you," Braydon bit out.

"Hen was determined to go, whether I went with her or not. Seemed the better choice," Percy said. "For all the help I was."

Just then they were interrupted by Bishop with the first aid kit.

"It's not like you to get jumped that way. Either of you," Brody said.

"I'm afraid a bit too much making merry at the wedding earlier left my reflexes a tad dulled," Percy said with a hangdog expression. "I know better."

"You two quit badgering Sir Percy," Laura said. "Let Bishop take a look. It might need a stitch."

Percy tried to leap to his feet but was held in place by Benjamin and Barron. "No needles," he said in a panicky voice.

"Nothing to worry about, Sir Percy," Barron said. "Bishop has fixed me up after a fight more times than I can count. He knows what he's doing."

"Good heavens. I hope you're not still fighting."

Barron shook his head. "No need these days. Unless, of course, I'm provoked."

The room fell silent as Bishop performed his magic, swabbing and then stitching up the gash on Percy's temple. Percy winced and turned white but didn't move a muscle until it was all over.

"This'll smart some," Bishop warned, daubing the wound with a clean cloth soaked in some of his magic elixir. "But it'll help it heal faster."

"I hardly felt that," Percy said.

"Got me some concoction made from wild herbs that helps dull the nerves below the skin."

"Thank you," Percy said to Bishop. "You're a handy fellow to know."

Bishop grinned as he packed up the first aid supplies. "Like I said, practiced lots on my brother over the years. Couldn't have him all scarred up. Make it too easy for folks to tell us apart."

"Back to the men who jumped you and grabbed Henrietta— any idea where they were coming from?" Braydon asked.

"It was dark, of course, but from what I could tell," Percy said, "it looked like they were coming from the ranch here."

Braydon and Brody exchanged looks. "Blake, you stay here with Laura and Percy. Don't open the door unless you're sure it's one of us. The rest of you, let's get out there and have a look around."

Henrietta was more riled by the fact that the bandits had taken off with her favorite mount than at being left tied up on the side of the road like last week's road-kill. Plus, they'd taken her rifle.

"And live to make them sorry, I will!" She spoke aloud, finding comfort in her own voice as she scrabbled around in the loose debris at the side of the road. After sifting through a few handfuls of nothing but dust, she finally found a rock with a pointed end. It took several tries to saw through her bonds. Luckily, the thieves had used an old piece of frayed rope, and before too long, she felt her wrists released as the final strands of jute gave way. She'd seen one of them give Percy a good wallop, but her friend was tough.

She gave her wrists a quick rub to get the circulation going as she made her way to her feet and bent down to retrieve her pistol from her boot. Only a fool would be out here unarmed after dark. Especially this close to Hawkes's spread.

She'd heard Hawkes's name muttered among the thugs as they debated what to do with her. Two of them seemed to think Hawkes would be delighted if they delivered her to his door, but the other two were smarter and ran the show. She shuddered, remembering how the fat one had wanted to keep her, one meaty hand on the swell of her bosom. Luckily, the others put him straight real fast.

She dusted herself off and started down the road to where they'd been set upon, then stopped. The buffoons had pulled off the road and out of sight just as the Masons' buckboard came around the bend on the way home from the wedding. She'd recognized the wagon in the dim twilight, even though the knife at her throat had prevented her from calling out.

With any luck, the Masons had scooped Percy up and

taken him to the ranch. No need for her to show up at the Copper Moon ranch, all bedraggled and victimized and on foot. She could hear Braydon Mason laughing already.

With new determination, she turned around and headed back the way she'd come. Back to Bullet. If nothing else, she'd set about getting their horses back.

ALL WAS quiet as the brothers mounted up and headed toward Bullet. Braydon, in the lead, noticed Hawkes's place stood in darkness. Had the thugs who attacked Percy and Henrietta been on his payroll? Or was there more than one gang of no-gooders taking up residence in Bullet? And if so, what was their intention with Henrietta? Maybe they'd try to unload her with Hawkes. He bit back a smile, pretty sure the poor bastards were already having second thoughts about having taken her with them.

The five of them arrived in Bullet without incident. Their surroundings grew livelier as they made their way down Main Street where light spilled from several windows and doorways. They passed the café, which lay in darkness, but Braydon was betting some of the wedding guests had taken themselves off to the saloon to continue the celebration. Music could be heard from several different sources, drowning out the raucous laughter and the furtive scurry of boot heels against wooden sidewalks.

"Holy!" Benjamin said, from his left. "It's been a long time since I've been in town on a Saturday night."

"This is nothing," Braydon scoffed. "Get yourself off to Yuma one evening. Now there's a party town."

"You can have it," Benjamin said, his gaze following Braydon's. "No sign of life at the café."

"What did you expect? Clearly, spinster Georgina needs her beauty rest."

"I thought she looked pretty today," Benjamin said.

Braydon turned away. Benjamin knew diddly about women and he was plumb tired of trying to educate him and the others. Let them find out the hard way about the fairer sex.

"What do you think, Brody?" he asked.

"If the men who attacked Percy and Henrietta are still in Bullet, bets are good they'll be in the saloon. Otherwise they kept going to Yuma."

"Or stopped at Hawkes's," Barron said. "Got a funny feeling this is all on him."

Braydon turned toward the twins. The two of them had a vested interest in seeing Hawkes brought to dust. Hawkes had killed their older brother. They had all been there and seen it happen, powerless to stop it. But it was something none of them would ever forget. The need to avenge that killing, to slowly and painfully destroy Hawkes, bonded them together thicker than any blood.

Braydon pulled up his mount and waited on Brody's decision. Did they check out the saloon or turn around?

Brody sighed. "I was hoping we'd come across Henrietta on the way here."

"They must have gagged her," Braydon said. "Otherwise she'd have screamed the town down by now. If they even got this far." Somehow, the thought of Henrietta being gagged and manhandled by a gang of thugs didn't bring him the satisfaction he might have expected. The thought of any man's hands on the feisty she-cat ... He gave his head a shake.

"We're looking for a needle in a haystack," Bishop said.

"Strangers here stick out like a sore thumb," Brody said.

"Check out the saloon?" Braydon asked.

Brody pointed to the twins. "You two go. Benjamin go with them. Keep them in line." He punctuated his words with a grin so they knew he was just kidding. "Braydon and I'll stay out here with the horses."

No one argued when Brody gave orders. They learned over the years it was far easier to follow along. Nowadays, they had Laura to call on as the voice of reason if they felt Brody was barking up the wrong tree.

"You okay, Bray?" Brody asked once they were alone.

"Sure thing. Why?"

"No special reason. Saw you sparring with Henrietta at the wedding earlier. Wanted to make sure you're not getting your tail feathers in a knot over this latest development. Nothing good ever comes when a man's head isn't level on his shoulders."

Braydon bit back a laugh. "What? You think I have feelings for Henrietta and likely to go off half-cocked and do something stupid because of it? She tossed her drink in my face."

Brody gave him a searching look from beneath the brim of his hat. "You wouldn't be the first man to up and do something stupid because a woman was involved."

"No worries there. I have no feelings toward the aforesaid lady except the urge to clap a hand over her mouth and shut her the hell up."

"Which is exactly how I feel about you, Braydon Mason."

"What the—" Braydon spun around in his saddle. His jaw dropped. Out of the dark shadows in the middle of the street, Henrietta rode into view with a second horse behind her. "We were told you'd been kidnapped."

Henrietta tossed her head. "Not for long. I came to

reclaim my horse and Percy's. No one gets away with taking what's mine."

Braydon had never been at a loss for words before, so was relieved when Brody jumped in. "Where are the men who hit Percy and grabbed you up?"

"Passed out back of the saloon. Is Percy okay?"

"Bishop patched him up. He'll have a headache but should be fine," Brody said.

"Okay, well, I'm going home." She turned her mount around. "Tell him I'll bring his horse out to the ranch at first light. From there we'll head out to our camp."

Brody dismounted and tied his horse to the hitching post alongside the others. "I'll go collect up the brothers. Braydon, you make sure the lady gets home safe."

Braydon looked to the backside of Henrietta's mount, as she headed off. "But Brody—"

"Go along now. It's the gentlemanly thing to do. She's been through a lot."

Braydon knew better than to argue. Once Brody's mind was made up, it would take a snowball melting in hell to change it. Or Laura. Only she wasn't here right now to take his side. Touching his heels to the horse's flanks, he started after Henrietta.

He caught up to her easily, just as she turned onto the side street where she and Percy had rented Amanda's house as a base for their so-called treasure hunt. Personally, he didn't believe there was a lick of treasure here in Bullet or anyplace else in Arizona. All the treasure was out west or up north in the gold mining towns.

Some days he'd love to just light out of here and join the quest. Then he'd remember his family and the pledge they'd made to take care of Hawkes once and for all.

Henrietta spared him the barest glance as he reached her side. "I don't need an escort home."

"Brody seems to think otherwise."

"Brody's just being overprotective because I rescued his wife one time."

"And he's still expressing his gratitude. We all are." The street was deserted, the houses they passed in darkness. Brody had to marvel at a woman like Henrietta, confident enough to be out here on her own after what happened earlier.

Most of the women he knew would be pulling the helpless damsel act, making him feel like they'd never have managed without him. Henrietta was nothing like those ladies. "Acting the big brother is kind of what Brody does."

"Same way as irritating folks is what you do?"

He bit back a smirk. Hard to say why he enjoyed getting her riled, but it gave him a great deal of pleasure. "You're wrong on that count. Charming the ladies is my particular specialty."

Henrietta snorted. "Save your charm."

While they were speaking, they'd reached the fenced backyard of Amanda's family home. Henrietta opened the gate and, once inside, dismounted.

Braydon followed suit. His actions were instinctive. There was no reason for him not to turn around and head back to the ranch except he needed to be close to her. Needed to meet her on her own ground.

"Get back on your horse, Braydon Mason. You've seen me home."

"Somehow, I think Brody meant for me to see you safely inside the house. Check around for intruders."

"Don't you get it? I can take care of myself."

"I'm sure you can. It's just, somedays, it's nice not to have to."

She pushed past him. "Spare me your charming ways. Save them for some woman who appreciates them."

"You've got no worries there. I mean, it's pretty clear you don't have a single ladylike bone in your body."

"Is that a fact?"

In a thrice, Henrietta pressed herself tight against him, wrapped her arms around his neck, and molded her lips to his.

CHAPTER 3

Braydon registered the fact that Henrietta felt a hell of a lot curvier than she looked in her modified man trousers and shapeless shirt. Her breasts were soft and inviting against his chest, kind of like her lips were on his. He was just starting to enjoy the way her mouth was exploring his, when she ended the kiss.

"Hmmph." Henrietta tilted her face up, as if studying him in the dim moonlight. "I kind of thought, given the way you talk, that you'd be a better kisser."

He didn't dignify her words with an answer, even as he was plotting out his next move. To have her back in his arms, begging for more.

Something of what he was thinking must have shown in his face, for she quickly put several arms' length between them before she started to remove the bridle for her horse.

He moved to Percy's horse and began to do the same.

"I told you I don't need your help," Henrietta said.

"Anyone ever tell you it's rude to turn down a helping hand when it comes your way? The boys and I weren't in town for our health tonight. We were looking to find you.

Had a plan to get you away from your assailants. Make sure you were safe."

Henrietta stopped what she was doing and turned to face him. A beam of moonlight illuminated one half of her face, accentuating the defined cheekbones, full lips, and stubborn jaw. He saw her mouth move as if framing her words before she spoke. He wanted to kiss her again, properly this time. But he was a big believer in choosing his moment.

"I'm not someone who typically needs to be rescued," she said. "But you're right. Please tell Brody and the others that I'm grateful you all cared enough to come after me."

"Tell' em yourself," Braydon said. He quickly finished seeing to the horse, removed the animal's saddle, and filled its feedbag with fresh oats.

"Thank you for your help," Henrietta said. He had a feeling the words were difficult for her to say aloud. "I can take things from here."

"Fair enough." Not being one to linger where he clearly wasn't welcome, Braydon mounted up. He paused before he left the yard. "What did the thieves get away with?"

"Only my rifle. The saddle bags were untouched."

"Would you recognize them again?"

"Without a doubt," Henrietta said. "What did you have in mind?"

"Nothing yet. But Brody and the rest of us, we're not too fussy on outsiders coming here and stirring things up."

"Does that include Percy and myself?"

Braydon blew out an exasperated breath. "That's not what I meant at all. I was referring to folks breaking the law. Usually because they know they can get away with it."

"Like Hawkes," she said.

"Like Hawkes," Braydon agreed. "Nothing much

happens around here that doesn't have his dirty paw print all over it. Got us a feeling those men who grabbed you up might have been working for him."

"I did hear them mention his name," she said. "Why would he care what Percy and I are up to?"

Braydon cocked her a look. "You and Sir Percy find a fortune in pearls out there, Hawkes will be more than a threat."

That said, Braydon left before he changed his mind. He had a feeling it would be quite a feat to convince Henrietta she was in need of any sort of protecting. And truth told, she needed protecting from him most of all. Because, damned if he didn't love a challenge!

THE BROTHERS WERE STILL UP, gathered around the kitchen table when he got back. Seeing him return, Brody rolled easily to his feet and plopped his hat on his head. "Time I turned in," he said, to no one in particular.

"I hope you weren't waiting up for me," Braydon said with a smirk. "If things had gone a little further, you might not have seen me till morning."

"Just glad to see you weren't making a nuisance and taking advantage of Miss Henrietta's shaken-up state after her ordeal," Brody said.

"Sending Braydon to look in on a lady," Benjamin said. "Kind of like sending the fox into the hen house, isn't it?"

The others guffawed.

Brody spoke up. "I have the feeling Miss Henrietta's more than capable of giving as good as she gets. Isn't that so, Percy?"

"Henny's been known to hold her own," Percy said.

"She sure was holding me," Braydon said, making a gesture with his hands. "Got this close to plant one on me."

Percy raised a brow. "Henny kissed you? You must have pissed her off some."

Braydon answered with a cocky smile. "Not my fault if the ladies find me irresistible."

"Make no mistake, my good fellow. Henrietta is not like most women."

"Which is exactly what intrigues me about her."

Brody turned to Percy. "Take my old room at the top of the steps. Henrietta said she'd be here bright and early."

"First light if I know her. Good night, all," Percy said, smothering a yawn. "Just one question, if I may."

"What's that?" Brody said.

"You're not really brothers, as least most of you aren't. How is it you all have the same last name?"

"Most of us were born with no last name," Braydon said lightly. "We thought it a nice tribute to take on Brody's, seeing as how he took on the lot of us."

"Very good," Percy said as he turned and made his way up the steps.

Braydon took the chair vacated by Percy.

Blake skewered him with a look. "So the lady's a bit of a fan, is she, Bray?"

Braydon didn't even try to look modest. "Could say. Had a fair bit of trouble keeping her hands to herself. And that's for sure."

"You always say that," Blake said. "How about you put a little money on it this time?"

"Yeah," Bishop said. "A little friendly wager between the five of us."

"What?" Braydon said. "A wager that I have her eating out of my hand in no time?"

Barron nodded. "How about before we're back from Cali?"

Blake chimed in. "I'm not going on this cattle drive. I can vet the results. Announce the winner when you boys get back."

"What kind of money are we talking?" Bishop said.

Braydon narrowed his eyes. The twins had been successful con artists before coming to Copper Moon, and they still loved a good wager. He sat back in his chair. "Tell you what. I'll throw in my cut of the profits from this next trip west if I haven't charmed Miss Henrietta to the point where she's crazy in love with me."

"Wa-hoo!" The twins hollered, slapped their hands on the table top and stamped their booted feet against the floor.

"I'll take that wager," Benjamin said. The others agreed with a handshake.

"Blake, you're on your honor to report your findings fairly," Braydon said.

"And no making stuff up," Benjamin said. "I wonder if we should get a second judge to keep things fair. Like Miss Georgina."

"You can't be telling the ladies," Barron said. "They stick together. They'd be tipping Miss Henrietta off as to what's going on."

"And we can't tell Brody," Bishop said.

"Why not?" Blake said. "Brody's the biggest gambler of any of us."

"Laura made him swear off the gambling when they got married," Braydon said. "Tell you what, though. Bradley will be back the day after next. He can keep an impartial accounting and see if it matches what Blake says."

Braydon reached out to the center of the table with his

right hand. One by one the others reached in for a group handshake.

Braydon sat back smugly. "Looking forward to collecting my winnings, boys."

~

HENRIETTA ARRIVED at the Copper Moon ranch before sun up. Even though she was early, there were already signs of life around the tidy ranch. Chickens ran around and scratched in the dirt, while a rooster strutted his stuff and heralded the start of a new day.

Henrietta tore her gaze from where the main ranch house squatted in the forefront of the driveway to the two smaller, new-looking cabins perched a short distance apart, in the area between the ranch house and outbuildings, close to the well.

Brody and Laura had moved into the first cabin after they were married. When Bradley and Amanda announced they were getting hitched, the brothers had hastily started work on a second cabin. She understood it had been finished right before the wedding yesterday, and was ready for the newlyweds to move into.

She wondered if the brothers would construct more cabins as more of them took the plunge. She could envision the compound in the not-too-distant future with kids running wild among the farm animals, the women worn ragged from childbearing and looking after the menfolk. She shuddered.

Back home in Argentina, every time one of her brothers had gotten married, he and his bride had moved into the family homestead on the vineyard. Even though they had servants to help out, it all ended up being extra work for Madre. A life Henrietta had narrowly escaped.

Thank goodness for her grandmother in England— the first stepping-stone to her life of independence and adventure.

Living here on the Copper Moon ranch, even in Bullet itself, must be stifling. At least Laura wouldn't be the only woman here once Amanda returned from her short honeymoon. Still, all those men underfoot. It was far too reminiscent of Henrietta's earlier life with her father and nine brothers in a country where women had no say and very little respect.

She rode up to the front of the ranch house and dismounted. "I knew you'd be here bright and early," Percy said from the open doorway.

Henrietta stepped inside cautiously, relieved to see they were alone. She had no wish to run into Braydon after kissing him last night. She still didn't understand what crazy impulse had sparked her actions. "Where is everyone?"

"Three of the boys are rounding up the herd to drive them to California. I guess the others are helping."

Henrietta kept her tone casual. "Who all's going?"

"Benjamin and the twins. Brody doesn't like to leave the ranch, Laura being in a family way and all."

"And the others?" she asked.

"Bradley will be away another day or two. Which leaves Blake and Braydon to stay behind and hold the place down with Brody."

"I see." She gave Percy a critical look. "You still look a little pale. How's your head?"

"I'm fine. Braydon said you got away easily last night. No repercussions?"

Henrietta snorted. "He wasn't the one trussed up alongside the road like buzzard bait. I managed to get myself free, then walk into town. Luckily our accosters were still there so I could reclaim our horses. They didn't empty our saddlebags or anything, but the bastards have my rifle."

"Lucky it wasn't your only one. Any clue who they were?"

"I've never seen them before. But I'd know them if I happened across them again." She faced Percy. "You ready?"

He made an ushering gesture. "Ladies first."

They hadn't ridden far before she pulled up short so she was facing Percy. "You and I have known each other a long time now. Long enough for me to know when there's something you're not telling me."

Percy made a guilty face as he pulled up his mount as well. "Only because I'm debating if you'd be better off not knowing."

"You know that's a crock. Now out with it!"

"I turned in last night before the others, due to my head aching and all." At her look, he made a deprecating face. "All right. Coupled with the overindulgence of spirits at the wedding celebration." He took a breath. "It wasn't long after, I got woken up by all the noise they were making downstairs."

"And you overheard something," Henrietta said. "Something you weren't supposed to hear."

"In a manner of speaking," Percy said.

"Hard to fathom they'd be having a secret conversation," Henrietta said.

"Secret from Brody, too," Percy said.

"Something he needs to know, that you need to tell him?"

"Not exactly," Percy said. "The conversation I overheard concerns you."

Henrietta straightened in the saddle. "What about me?"

Percy blew out a breath. "It would seem Braydon is planning to come wooing, hat in hand, in an effort to win you over."

"I don't believe you," she said. Even as she spoke, she couldn't help but wonder. He had been a little too helpful last evening.

"It's true. He claimed he'd have you fawning over his every move by the time the others get back. The brothers made a wager he'll fall flat."

"He has no hope," Henrietta said flatly. "It's nothing but a waste of his time and money."

"I thought I ought to tell you, anyway. I have a feeling Braydon can be extremely charming when he puts his mind to it."

Henrietta kneed her horse a little harder than intended. "Do you really think you need to warn me not to succumb to his charms?"

"I'm just telling you, whatever his line of patter, it's not sincere. I don't want to see you getting hurt again, Hen."

HAWKES WOKE up to a pounding in his skull and a thousand fiery pins of light digging behind his eyelids. He threw an arm across his eyes in an attempt to make it all go away. His back and neck stabbed him in protest at the movement.

"Aren't you one sorry sight." The light intensified with the sound of drapes being opened. Moving was torture as he slowly swung his legs over the side of the settee where he had spent the night, and eased to a sitting position. He opened his eyes and forced his bleary gaze to focus on his visitor. Make that two visitors. Don Lucas and Saunders, his solicitor.

"What the hell?" he snarled, through a mouthful of marbles.

"We let ourselves in," Don Lucas said, in his smoothly accented English. "It seems to be the help's day off."

"Got no help," Hawkes muttered. "Bunch of unreliable greasers. Fired' em all."

He was aware of the way Saunders and Lucas exchanged a look.

"You should be more careful," Saunders said. "Anyone could come in at any time when you're in this condition. We don't need snoops and spies getting wind of what we're about."

"'s taken care of." Hawkes spoke around the hunk of dry flannel pretending to be his tongue. His mouth was dry as the desert. He fumbled on a nearby table, and his fist closed around a sticky glass with a small measure of whiskey. He latched on and swallowed gratefully. The whiskey burned the back of his parched throat.

"Water!" he croaked.

"You're a sorry sight," Don Lucas said, not an ounce of pity in his voice.

"You missed our meeting in my office this morning," Saunders said.

Hawkes squinted past them toward the window and the bright ball of light in the sky. Had to be past noon. "So?" he said belligerently.

"The assayer and his team are out on the Copper Moon. We don't want the Masons to accidentally stumble across them."

"They're supposed to be driving the herd west," Hawkes said. "Which leaves the ranch free and clear."

"Yes, some of them are undertaking that journey. But they never all leave the ranch at once. We've also got that snoopy Brit and his sidekick out there, searching around for God only knows what," Don Lucas said. "Sunken treasure, according to local gossip. It would be most unfortunate if those two ran across our team of experts and reported back to the Masons about the sudden interest in the back forty of their spread."

"Took care of them two the other night," Hawkes said.

"Not well enough, from what I hear around town," Lucas said. "The girl got free and had the balls to follow your men to Bullet on foot. The Masons weren't far behind her."

"They don't know dick. None of them," Hawkes said. "Just some roadside robbery."

"None-the-less," Saunders said. "Clean yourself up and take yourself out to have a little chat with our British friend. You can be all concerned about the robbery and such. Make sure him and his whore stay well away from where the vein of copper runs through the ranch."

Hawkes lumbered to his feet. "Get the hell out! I gotta go take a piss."

Don Lucas gave a disdainful sniff. "It smells like you already have."

Hawkes looked down. Sure enough, there was a wet patch on the front of his trousers. Damn shame when a man had no privacy in his own home.

Saunders gave him a disgusted look. "What happened to you in prison, Guy?"

"You don't wanna know."

"Whatever happened, I suggest you forget it and move on. Don Lucas and I would appreciate having our friend and business partner back."

"Easy for you to say," Hawkes mumbled to the empty

doorway as the men left. "Damn those Masons all to hell. Damn the whole world!"

～

HENRIETTA WAS EXCITED to get back to their base camp. They'd been following Percy's mapping of what the area most likely looked like a hundred and fifty years earlier, when salt water basins were periodically connected to the river. At that time, a high tidal bore could conceivably carry a ship far off course through the salt marshes, only to get landlocked once the tides receded and the marshes dried out.

She knew Percy was methodical in his research and the promise of finding Spanish explorer Juan de Iturbe's ship filled with rare black pearls was the most exciting treasure hunt she'd been on so far.

They'd erected a big old canvas tent furnished with two cots to protect them from the heat and the bugs. A lot of treasure hunters travelled with an entourage of servants and workers, but when she met Percy, he preferred to work alone. It had taken some doing to persuade him to let her accompany him and help with some initial exploratory digs in different countries.

She filled several canteens while Percy pored over his papers, trying to pinpoint the exact location where the ship might have ended up. "I'm going out to collect some soil and sand samples," she said as she mounted up. "Once we get them analyzed for salt, it should tell us if we're anywhere near close."

Percy barely glanced up and nodded absentmindedly before he returned to his papers. Henrietta smiled as she mounted up. She and Percy made a good team. He thrived on the historical research and puzzle-solving involved in treasure-hunting, while she preferred the physical activity of being out grubbing around in the wild looking for clues.

Before she'd come to Yuma, Henrietta had assumed one desert was pretty much the same as the next, but nothing could be further from the truth. Egypt was thousands of years old, rife with centuries of history going back to before Christ. The American colonies, on the other hand, comprised a country in its infancy, still finding its identity.

In a land raw and untamed, yet teeming with possibilities, she could see the attraction for the early settlers who came here to make their mark. Very different from Argentina, where generation after generation stayed put, worked the land, and continued to build the legacy started by their ancestors.

Because of its proximity to the Colorado River, the desert here wasn't as barren as those on the other side of the world. And no matter how empty of life the landscape appeared on the surface, she knew it was home to a myriad of creatures, most of whom came out at night when it was cooler.

She collected a variety of soil and sand samples, carefully marking each location before linking the location with the individual sample sealed in its glass jar.

She was heading back to base camp when she caught sight of movement out of her periphery vision, over near a rocky cliff. She stopped, shaded her gaze, but all remained still. Could her eyes have been playing tricks? She didn't think so. Remembering what had happened the other evening, her and Percy being accosted by those strange men, sent a chilly warning shiver trickling down her side, despite the heat.

As tempting as it was to go explore the spot where she'd

seen something moving, she turned the other way toward base camp. Percy was alone. For that matter, so was she. She hated the sudden feeling of vulnerability that swept through her. Being alone never used to bother her.

As the camp became visible, she saw a strange horse tied up near their tent. Quietly, she dismounted a short distance away to travel the rest of the distance on foot, rifle at the ready. Stealthily, she circled the camp. As she drew close, she heard the rise and fall of men's voices, their words indistinguishable. The hair on the back of her neck prickled a warning seconds before a large, gloved hand was clapped across her mouth.

CHAPTER 4

"Ssshhh," hissed a familiar male voice in her ear. A voice that caused her heartbeat to quicken and her pulse to slow. Henrietta relaxed her grip on her gun.

"Hawkes is over there with Percy," Braydon said. "Was he expected? I thought you two were poison to him after you intervened when he tried to kidnap Laura and Amanda."

Definitely there was no love lost between Hawkes and her or Percy. Any more than there was between her and Braydon. She reached up and tugged his hand away from her mouth. Her lips throbbed from the recent pressure. "What are you doing out here?" she whispered.

"I was worried about you two after what happened the other night. Thought I'd mosey out this way to make sure everything was okay. I was on my way when I spotted Hawkes headed here, so I fell back and circled around."

Belatedly, Henrietta remembered the wager Percy had told her about between Braydon and the others. Her lips softened in a smug half smile. Could this be his way of seeking her out as the first step in his attempt to woo her?

Braydon was watching her closely. "Something tickle your funny bone?"

She tilted her head and gave him what she hoped was a beguiling smile. "Just you. Being so cute and worried and all." She rested her free hand on his chest and felt the warmth of his skin through the fabric of his shirt. "Percy knows what he's about with Hawkes. Keeping him updated. Or so Hawkes thinks. That way Hawkes leaves us alone."

"Didn't seem that way the other night. Not if Hawkes was behind you two getting jumped."

Braydon gave a puzzled frown, and she removed her hand from his chest. No point in raising his suspicions by being too friendly. "We don't know for sure those men were working for Hawkes. They could have been just petty thieves casing out the area, and panicked when we came along."

His gaze narrowed. "You said you heard them mention Hawkes's name." She forgot she had told him that part. "I said it sounded like they mentioned Hawkes. I could have been mistaken."

He tensed at the sign of sudden movement near the tent, then blew out a breath as Hawkes and Percy appeared and shook hands.

"Told you," she said. "Percy likes to keep his friends close and his enemies closer. Hawkes thinks he's got a stake in whatever treasure we find. Percy lets him think that."

"Percy doesn't know the dangerous game he's playing where Hawkes is concerned. The man knows no loyalty. Killed his wife and drove his own son away after he disowned him. And he certainly never forgets anyone who crosses him."

"Seems he's been keeping his distance since he got out of jail."

"Biding his time is more like it. Plotting his revenge against those of us who put him there in the first place."

"Why do I have a feeling it goes further back than that?" Henrietta asked.

"Because you're smart. And you're right. Come on, he's gone."

Before she could take a step forward, he clasped her hand in his, the rough, time-worn leather of his glove abrading the smooth skin on the back of her hand.

Yesterday she would have pulled away. But not today. Today, she intended to take full advantage of what Percy had told her about Braydon's wager with his brothers. Let Braydon think he was winning her over.

Percy was back hunched over his papers by the time she and Braydon cleared the cottonwoods and circled the tent to the front. He looked up and frowned when he saw Henny's hand tucked up in Braydon's.

As if he sensed Percy's disapproval, Braydon released her.

"Is something wrong?" Percy asked. "Where's your horse?"

"Relax," Henrietta said. "He's back there with Braydon's. The two of them are getting to know each other."

"Did you get the samples all right?"

Henrietta nodded. "I thought I'd head back to town and start the analysis. What did I miss here?"

Percy lowered his gaze to the papers in front of him. "Not a thing." He shot Braydon a hard look. "What brings you out this way?"

"Just checking to make sure you two are all right," Braydon said easily. "Ran into Henny on her way back."

Percy harrumphed.

"Since everything's in order, I guess I'll accompany

Henrietta back to town. You'll be okay here by yourself?" Braydon asked.

"Why wouldn't I be?" Percy asked, defensively.

Henrietta wasn't used to seeing Percy so evasive.

"Just wanted to make sure you've not had any unwanted visitors," Braydon said.

"Out here? Are you mad? What would anyone be doing out here?"

Braydon's glance swept the area. "Can't help thinking the place is hiding its share of secrets."

"Like the whereabouts of the pearl ship. That's the only secret we care to unearth. Isn't that right, Hen?"

She nodded absently, her mind still back on the movement she'd seen near the cliffs. It hadn't been Braydon and it hadn't been Hawkes. So who or what had she seen?

BRAYDON REMAINED on his best behavior as he saw Henrietta back to town. He felt her grow tense as the house drew into sight. Was she fixing to repeat their kiss from last night? Or was she worried he might try to take things a step further? Having her on her guard would thwart his plans.

He pulled up his horse as they reached the gate into the yard and tipped his hat in her direction. "I'll say good-bye, then. I know you have work to do. I'll stop by later and check on you."

Expecting an argument at that last, he was dumbfounded by her response. She leaned across her saddle toward him. Close enough that he could catch a teasing whiff of her clean, floral fragrance. Close enough that he could see the many different shades of green in her irises, and the thick, dark fan of her lashes.

"I'll look forward to that, Braydon." Her horse trotted past his before he could frame a response. He seemed to always be talking to the back of her horse.

"Maybe, if you're in the mood, we could mosey up to the café and grab a bite later."

She turned. "I believe Georgina closed today so they could clean up after the wedding. Why don't I make us something to have here later?"

His jaw dropped. "I, uh ... That sounds nice. Real nice."

She dismounted and flashed him a pretty smile. "Good. See you later, then."

Braydon shook his head as he turned in the direction of the ranch. A little, niggly suspicion prickled the back of his neck. Henrietta was not acting true to character. Something was up with her. And wouldn't it be fun to find out what that something was.

All thoughts of the intriguing puzzle that was Henrietta faded when Braydon reached the ranch. Brody and Blake were out front, alongside their next-door neighbor, Ross. Judging from the body language, it did not appear to be a social visit.

Braydon knew Brody had loaned the other rancher money from time to time to pay his taxes, with no expectation of repayment anytime soon. The Rosses had six little kids and no help, so eking out a living from their ranch was a constant struggle. Their spread was also too far from the river to take advantage of irrigation the way the Copper Moon did.

As he approached, Braydon saw Ross extending a packet in Brody's direction. He dismounted in time to hear Brody say, "I never wanted to be paid back, Ross. And certainly not like this."

"I told you I always pay my debts," Ross said. "Take the money, Brody. I tacked on interest."

"Must have been a darn good offer for the ranch," Brody said. "I wish you'd have come to me. I'd have matched it."

"I couldn't let you pay me more than it's worth," Ross said. "And that's what this group offered."

"Do you know who bought it?" Brody asked.

Ross shook his head. "Saunders brokered the deal for a group of investors. He hinted they seem to think that there's some sort of discovery in the works, like oil. Pipe dream, for sure. If there was oil to be found, you and I would have found it by now." He cleared his throat. "I gotta tell you, the missus is delighted. This life is too hard on her. She's right thrilled to be going back to Boston." He made a face. "What she calls civilization."

Brody shrugged as he accepted the money. "Ranching's in your blood, Ross. The city will choke the life out of you."

"Blood or not, I was never any good at it. Not the way you are. The way you turned around your uncle's sad-ass attempt at a ranch and made it into something."

"I had a lot of help," Brody said. "I would have preferred first refusal if I knew you were thinking of selling. You could have stayed on as partner."

Ross spat on the ground at his feet. "I've taken enough of your charity, Brody. It's time to move on. Past time."

Brody shook the other man's hand. "We'll miss you around here, and that's for sure."

Blake shook Ross's hand as well and Braydon moved in, figuring he'd better complete the circle. "Sorry to hear you're leaving."

Braydon stood in a half circle with the other two as Ross remounted and headed back down the driveway.

"We need to find out who he just sold to," Brody said once Ross was out of earshot.

"Whoever they claim to be," Braydon said, "you can bet Hawkes is in the thick of it. What was that crazy talk about oil?"

Brody's gaze didn't quite meet his. "Just that. Crazy talk."

LAURA LOOKED up from her reading when Braydon came down the stairs of the ranch house in his finest duds. Not his suit, but a fancy jacket, good pants, white shirt with a string tie, and his dress boots.

"You look pretty duded up for a night in Bullet," she said. "You headed into Yuma?"

"Nope. Have me a dinner date with a pretty gal right here in town."

"Anyone I know?"

"Matter of fact, you do know her."

Laura rested her magazine on her lap. "Oh?"

"Miss Henrietta happens to be the lucky lady who has the pleasure of my company for the evening."

"Henrietta?" Laura's brow furrowed. "Aren't you both like two mad cats, hissing and spitting every time you catch sight of the other?"

"No idea where you got that impression," Braydon said, wiping at an imaginary spot of lint on his sleeve.

"In that case, you best gather up a handful of those black-eyed Susans I planted over near the cabin. Ladies like flowers, you know."

He leaned over and pressed a kiss to the top of her head. "I'll do that, thanks. Got myself a pretty good idea of what the ladies like, you know."

"Just remember, Henrietta isn't like most ladies. She's lived a very independent life for the last ten years."

"And don't you forget," Braydon said as he plopped his hat on his head. "I was raised in a house full of very independent ladies."

"Just don't go mistaking Henrietta for the type of women you're accustomed to. I don't want to see you bringing home a black eye."

Braydon smiled and patted her stomach. "Won't we all be happy when you have yourself your own young one to worry over?"

"You boys will always be my brothers," Laura said. "Say hello to Henrietta for me. Tell her to pop by one of these days. I could use a dose of female company."

"I'll tell her."

It was a shame Ross sold out, Braydon thought as he passed the Rosses' place. It was no secret Hawkes had been trying for years to buy up everyone's ranch in these parts. Braydon had always chalked it up to Hawkes being a power-hungry son of a bitch. Could there be something to that talk of oil?

He dismissed the idea as soon as it rose. Given all those old salt marshes back there between them and the river it hardly seemed a likely spot to find oil.

Once he and the others had their way to destroying the man, maybe they could do something useful. Something to make Bullet a better place to live. With Hawkes out of the picture, and folks no longer quaking in their boots in case he took a pot shot at them, Bullet could turn out to be a darn nice place.

As he knocked on the door to Henrietta's, he wondered how their sleepy town stacked up against the exotic places she'd seen— Greece and Egypt, to name just a few. He hadn't seen much exotic about Mexico the times he'd been there picking up a herd of cattle. California though, that was kind of an interesting place.

Funny, he'd never had itchy feet. Maybe because his early years were anything but typical. These days, he enjoyed the warmth of security he'd found as part of the Mason clan.

Henrietta answered the door, a look of dismay on her face. "Don't tell me you forgot I was coming?" he said teasingly, as he passed her the bouquet of black-eyed Susans.

She took the flowers absently, then glanced over her shoulder to where a cloud of black smoke escaped from the stove.

"What the—" Braydon pushed past her. "Something's burning!"

"I know. It's our dinner." She laid the flowers on the table, which was set for two. "Totally ruined, I'm afraid."

Braydon grabbed a rag and wrenched open the oven door, coughing as a mass of black smoke hit him in the face. He reached in and pulled out the source of the smoke. Two steps took him to the back door, which he opened. He stepped out and flung the offending article into the night. He left the door open and waved the rag in an attempt to clear the smoke.

Once the air had cleared some, he turned back to Henrietta. "I'm afraid to ask what was going to be for dinner."

"I've never cooked a roast before. It always looked easy when Percy made one."

He cocked his head, a half smile tugging at one side of his mouth. "You telling me you can't cook?"

She shrugged. "I never learned. We had cooks at home when I was growing up. Had to with ten kids. Then I was in England with my grandmother, who was an awesome cook.

After that I was traveling. I got very good at ordering off a menu, even when I didn't speak the language."

"That's okay. I don't cook much either. Which is what happens when you grow up in a houseful of ladies who all took turns."

"Now what?" Henrietta asked.

Braydon saw he wasn't the only one who'd taken care with his appearance. Henrietta was wearing a striking emerald gown that brought out the green of her eyes. Her straight, dark hair, which she normally wore loose, was swept back into some kind of fancy rolled-up do. Lamp light glinted on the jeweled pins holding it in place.

"You look too good to stay in, anyway. What say we take ourselves into Yuma?"

IN NO TIME, Braydon had the buggy hitched and they were underway. "We could have ridden, you know," Henrietta said. "It would be faster than the buggy."

"There's no hurry. You look too pretty to be up in a saddle, and this way I get to sit next to you on the drive."

And here came that famous Braydon Mason charm again, rolling off his tongue in an attempt to snow her and render her helpless under the attention. Henrietta gritted her teeth and leaned in closer, allowing one hand to brush his masculine thigh as if accidentally. She felt the muscle tighten beneath her gloved fingertips.

"This is a lovely idea. I haven't been to Yuma other than when I got off the train and caught the coach to Bullet."

"Pretty typical western town," Braydon said. "Downright lively next to Bullet."

"And this is where you grew up?" she asked as he guided

the buggy down the main street in town. She saw a great many signs advertising various businesses, including a bank, a solicitor, a barber, a dance hall, a mercantile, a gentlemen's hat shop and a ladies' millinery and fashion.

"It was called Arizona City when I was in short pants. I still remember when the name of the town was changed to Yuma. Not long after that, they built the state prison on Twin Hill over there." She turned to look where he indicated but could only see a hulking shadow in the distance. He stopped the rig in front of the Savoy Hotel. "If I recall correctly, they serve a decent meal here."

"Whatever they serve, it will be a big improvement over burnt roast beef."

She waited as he jumped out, secured their horses, then came around to help her alight. She stood, expecting him to offer her a hand. Instead, his hands spanned her waist. He lifted her from the rig onto the street next to him as if she weighed no more than a feather.

His hands lingered on her waist longer than necessary or appropriate as he smiled down at her. Rather than step back, she rested her hands lightly atop his forearms and tilted her head to smile up at him. She'd never been one for flirting and teasing, so this new departure was kind of fun.

He tucked her arm into the crook of his elbow, resting his free hand atop hers as they made their way inside, where they were seated at a candle lit table by the window. The dining room was about half full, mostly low-voiced couples engaged in intimate conversations. Music from a lone pianist in the far corner added to the elegance of their surroundings.

The waiter arrived with the menus. "The trout is very good this evening, sir. As is the quail."

"Thank you," Braydon said. "I do believe a bottle of your

best Champagne is in order." He leaned toward her. "I seem to recall you like Champagne, Henrietta?"

She placed her napkin in her lap, not rising to his teasing. "Who doesn't like Champagne?"

Once the Champagne had been fetched and opened, the cork inspected and their glasses filled, Braydon raised his glass toward her. "To a special evening with a special lady."

Henrietta raised her glass. "To enjoying good company."

"I'll drink to that." Braydon continued to study her over the rim of his glass. "You look lovely tonight, by the way. The candlelight is kissing your skin." Henrietta heard, "the way I'd like to later," implied but unspoken.

Thank you." She noticed the way his lips caressed his glass and imagined them caressing her own lips instead. She might need to give that kissing experiment another try before the evening was over.

"May I presume to order for us both?" Braydon asked.

Henrietta bit back the retort that she was more than capable of ordering her own food, having done it on several different continents. "By all means."

The ordering out of the way, silence fell between them. "You have a most interesting family," she said when she could stand the silence no longer.

"Every family is different," Braydon said. "What is yours like? Are you close?"

She gave her head a brief shake. "I left home ten years ago. After nine boys, I think having a girl in the family was a difficult adjustment for everyone. I never quite fit in." She pressed her lips together as unwanted memories rose. The clumsy advances by their closest neighbor, for which she got blamed for acting too provocatively. Her father's attempt to marry her off and quiet the scandal. The lack of support from her mother, who was afraid of her husband. The reprieve orchestrated by her English grandmother. Apparently, her father owed the old lady money, and Grandmadre wasn't above leveraging that in exchange for her granddaughter.

"Any thoughts on going back? Even for a visit?"

"It's a long journey," Henrietta said.

"This from a woman who has journeyed to Egypt? Sounds like an excuse to me."

"I don't expect I would be welcome," Henrietta said. "I was accused of bringing shame to my family."

"Because you left?"

"No. Because I refused to marry the man my father chose. A man who tried to force himself on me."

Braydon sat back, fingers steepled. "No woman should have to suffer that." Henrietta could almost hear him reworking his strategy to woo her.

They were interrupted by the arrival of their meal, thus sparing her from any further personal questions.

Meal consumed, they were lingering over coffee when two women strolled past the window and stopped. Henrietta noticed both ladies were attractive, in the way of a mature woman fighting to hold on to her youth with the heavy use of cosmetics and finery. They both broke into smiles at the sight of Braydon, who gave them an acknowledging nod.

Minutes later, the women appeared at the doorway of the dining room. She overheard the host waiter, telling the pair in a rather loud voice that the restaurant was full, even though the room was dotted throughout with empty tables.

"Excuse me." Braydon put down his napkin, stood, and approached the man who was attempting to deny the women entrance. "These two ladies are my guests, and there is plenty of room at my table for them." Even from a distance, Henrietta could see the waiter was unhappy about the turn of events. "But, sir —"

"But nothing," Braydon said, as he took one arm of each lady. "Kindly bring a second bottle of Champagne and four glasses."

Henrietta stood as the three-some made their way toward her. "Henrietta, please meet Missy and Cindy, two special ladies who washed my mouth out with soap a time or two in my youth."

"No doubt it was warranted," Henrietta said. "Pleasure to meet you both. Please sit down."

"We don't want to interrupt. We just wanted to stop in and say hello to Braydon. He doesn't pop by nearly as much as he used to."

"Please," Henrietta said. "We've finished our meal and I would love nothing more than to hear some delightfully scandalous stories about Braydon in his youth."

"Oh, he was a handful, all right," Missy said as she settled into an empty chair and shrugged out of her wrap. "Even as a lad he had too much charm for his own good."

"Spoiled to boot," Cindy added, fluffing her hair beneath her flamboyant hat. "We're all to blame for that."

"And why was that?" Henrietta asked.

"Poor little tyke," Cindy said. "Grew up never knowing who his mother was."

CHAPTER 5

"Thank you so much for a most enjoyable evening," Henrietta said as Braydon delivered her safely to her front door. "I had a good time."

He gave her a rueful smile. "No doubt you did. Being regaled by humiliating stories of my youthful escapades."

She couldn't hold back her smile. "I did get to see a whole different side of you."

"I hope it wasn't too off-putting."

"On the contrary, I was most impressed by the way you put that snotty maître d' in his place."

"I hate seeing people being treated badly due to their station in life," Braydon said. "Along with folks being treated like royalty when they don't deserve it."

"Is it true you don't know who your mother is? I find that hard to believe. Someone must know."

"Oh, Zara's ladies who were there at the time all knew who she was," Braydon said. "They made a pact to keep her identity secret."

Henrietta pondered that. Her family had been difficult,

but at least she knew where she came from. "Does it bother you not knowing?"

"I got teased a lot at school because of where I lived. The teachers weren't much better, looking down their nose at me. I came to terms with the situation years ago. Besides, there are far more pressing concerns at the moment."

Henrietta knew he was going to kiss her well before it happened.

First, he put one finger under her chin and tipped her face up. Making a loose fist, he ran his knuckles over her cheekbone to her jaw, then lightly brushed her lips with his fingertips. All the while he was providing her lots of time to step away.

His free hand tucked a loose tendril of hair behind her ear, tracing the shape of her ear with interesting results. Nerve endings she hadn't known existed were suddenly brought to life. Heat prickled in the most unlikely of places. The top of her legs. The backs of her knees.

She moistened her lips with the tip of her tongue, which seemed to be all the encouragement he needed.

"You kissed me last time. Now I'm going to show you how I kiss a lady."

The possessive purr of his words set her blood pounding and her heart racing. She all but held her breath, waiting. And damn him, he took his sweet time before he lowered his head and took possession of her mouth.

Skilled shaping of her lips beneath his softened her mouth and urged her lips to open for him. To allow him access to plumb the depths of her inner recesses.

The kiss was primal mating at its finest as his tongue found hers in a dance as old as time. Henrietta was drowning, caught in a vortex and swept away to a foreign place, a place where she needed more, wanted more.

Her fingers tangled through his thick dark hair as he branded her as his. A restless longing invaded her limbs as she rubbed against him. He shifted his stance, and one long leg nuzzled its way against hers. The insistent pressure of his hard muscles incinerated a heated need that flooded her limbs and stole her breath. His hands clasped her waist and angled her torso against his for a perfect fit.

He held her tight as he ended the kiss. How had he known her legs were like mush, unable to support her as she fought for breath?

"I have to hand it to you. No one has ever kissed me quite like that before." Why not let him have this tiny victory? She'd be better prepared next time, now that she knew how he played the game.

"I'd like to spend more time with you. With your approval, of course."

"Good," she said. "Come out to the base camp when you can spare the time. I'll be happy to put you to work."

"THINK you can manage without me for a couple of days?" Braydon asked Brody the next morning.

"That all depends. What's up?"

"Thought I might go help Percy at the camp for a few days," Braydon said casually.

"I don't suppose your sudden interest in hidden treasure has anything to do with Percy's right-hand-lady helper?"

"She is something of an enigma, that one. Taking a bit to get her figured out."

"And you never could resist a challenge, could you?" Brody said.

"Not one that concerns the fairer sex."

"One of these days, you're going to get bit bad, my friend." Brody clapped him on the back. "Which ought to be quite amusing to witness. In the meantime, fill your boots. Bradley and Amanda ought to be back later today from Yuma."

"Speaking of which ..." Braydon turned to see the newly-weds' horse and buggy coming down the driveway toward them. Bradley had barely pulled the rig to a stop before Amanda bounced out and made her way toward them without waiting for her groom.

Braydon noticed the happy flush heightening Amanda's naturally rosy coloring and guessed married life was agreeing with her. At least thus far.

"We had a most wonderful time." Amanda was fairly bubbling with news. "I brought Laura some new books to read from the mobile library."

"The what?"

"The mobile library. A covered wagon full of books that travels around the state. The most amazing woman runs it. Her name is Storm. Laura will love her. I told her she has to bring the library to Bullet and come out to visit us when she's here."

Bradley stood to one side, beaming indulgently as his new wife carried on three conversations at once, and no one could get a word in edgewise. Bradley had never been much of a talker, so Braydon guessed he was likely relieved to get back to the ranch and some male company.

"Place is still standing, I see," Bradley said, once he finally managed to get in a word. Laura must have heard the commotion, for she soon joined them.

Braydon noticed the way Brody looped an arm comfortably over his wife's shoulder and smiled down protectively.

Meanwhile, Amanda hung onto Bradley's arm and gazed adoringly up at him.

Glancing from couple to couple, Braydon felt strangely excluded from their happy little circle of marital bliss. He didn't like the feeling.

Ever since he hooked up with Brody and the others, he'd felt part of something special. Over the years, the seven of them had been an unstoppable force, helping to ensure Bullet was a safe town for all its inhabitants, with lots more work to do. Including running Hawkes into the ground so he never took out anyone again. Braydon hoped the recent inclusion of women into Copper Moon's male enclave wasn't about to suddenly change all that.

"Glad you're back, man," Brody said. "Bray has itchy feet to try his hand at treasure hunting with Percy and Miss Henrietta."

Laura gave Braydon a speculative glance. "Why do I suspect it might be something other than the buried treasure that's the attraction?"

Brody tapped his wife on the nose. "That's because you have a naturally suspicious nature, is all."

Laura addressed Braydon. "You should bring her back to the house for dinner one night. Poor thing probably never gets a home-cooked meal."

Braydon bit back a smile, recalling the charred roast beef threatening to ignite her oven. "You're probably right about that." He clapped Bradley on the back. "Good to have you back."

"You heading out now?"

"Tomorrow," Braydon said. After all, he didn't want to tip his hand by looking too anxious. He had less than a week to have Henrietta enslaved to him. Last night's kiss had felt like a good start. Judging from her reaction, the rest of the wooing ought to go pretty smooth.

HENRIETTA HAD BEEN on her guard ever since she returned to the base camp. The more she thought about what she had seen the other day, the more convinced she was that it had been a small group of men, obviously trespassing. She regretted not saying something to Braydon so he could in turn tell Brody, but Braydon had been catching her off guard lately far more than she was comfortable with, and the memory of shadowy movement near the cliffs had been far from the most important thing on her mind.

Thank goodness she knew about Braydon's wager with his brothers. Otherwise ... Otherwise she wasn't at all sure how she would have reacted to his overt and charming attention.

He certainly did have a way of gazing at a woman as if she was the only female in his universe. And the way he had championed those older ladies the night they were in Yuma had definitely tugged at her feminine sensibilities. He'd been more than kind, never once poking fun at her failed attempt at cooking. And then telling her he wanted to spend more time with her. Luckily, she knew his true intentions.

She'd been checking and re-checking Percy's calculations, but her mind was far away from the papers in front of her.

"Percy." She laid down her pencil and propped her chin in her hand, elbow resting on the oversize table they used as a desk.

Percy gave her a look. "I know your mind is miles away, Hen. Has been for several days now. Not on Braydon Mason,

I hope. Don't make me sorry I ever told you about that stupid wager he has with his brothers."

"He's not so bad," Henrietta said. She had to at least pretend she was falling for the scoundrel, and pulling the wool over the eyes of her best friend wouldn't be easy.

Percy gave her a sharp look. "Did something happen to change your mind from the way you were spitting at him the day of Bradley and Amanda's wedding?"

"Actually, something else has been bothering me. I saw Hawkes out here talking to you the other day, yet you didn't mention his visit."

"I didn't want to worry you. I have Hawkes handled."

Henrietta fell silent. "Did he mention if he was alone?"

"I didn't ask. He didn't offer. Why?"

"I was coming back from collecting the samples when I'm sure I saw someone, possibly more than one person, out near the cliffs."

"What would someone be doing out there? And why?"

"Hawkes thinks we're partners. But what if he's planning a double-cross?"

"Hen, I've been doing this a long time. A lot longer than you. When there are huge winnings at stake, you always have to be on guard for someone double-dealing behind your back. Hawkes is a prime example of someone to watch out for."

"So he could have spies out here."

"I'd be very surprised if he didn't."

"Speaking of spies, I invited Braydon Mason to come out and help us when he's able."

Percy gave her another sharp look. She responded with an innocent smile.

"Don't give me that innocent act. I know you too well. What exactly are you up to?"

"There was an increased salt content in that last sand sample I took back to town. I think it's time we cordoned off a dig site. It never hurts to have a pair of strong arms to help with the heavy work."

Despite her quick response, she could tell Percy didn't buy her pat answer for one second.

THE BASE CAMP was deserted when Braydon arrived the next morning, and immediately he thought the worst. Something had happened. Someone had kidnapped Percy and Henrietta.

Idiot, he told himself. *The two of them have hunted treasure all over the world.* They should certainly be able to take care of themselves in a small town like Bullet.

Yet, what of the thugs that accosted them the other night? Yes, it was a good thing he'd come out to check on them. He guided his horse in the direction of where he'd come across Henrietta the other day. He didn't like to admit to himself how much it bothered him, the thought of her being out here alone. Good thing he was around to keep an eye on her.

Except it wasn't Henrietta he finally came across, it was Percy. The man had a length of rope and some wooden stakes and was marking out a chunk of land that, far as Braydon could tell, looked just like the rest of the dried-up salt marsh desert that stretched for miles in every direction.

The man was red-faced and sweating as he toiled in the hot sun.

Braydon rode up to him. "Don't give yourself heat-stroke, Percy. You're not used to these temperatures."

Percy mopped his face with a handkerchief he pulled

from his back pocket. "I'll give you that, old boy. England it's not. About on a par with Egypt, actually."

Braydon glanced around, keeping his tone casual. "Where's Henrietta?"

Percy waved a vague hand. "Some bee in her bonnet about seeing someone the other day over near the cliffs. Wanted to go have a closer look. Tried to talk her out of it, but you know Hen when her mind is made up. Cussed stubborn."

"Sorely lacking common sense as well. She ought to have waited till I got here. I'd have gone with her to keep an eye out."

"I have never known Henrietta to wait for any man."

Braydon caught a bit of a warning in the other man's words as he indicated Percy's handiwork. "What's this all about?"

"This, my good man, is where I hope to find the missing ship of black pearls."

Braydon eyeballed the site. "How far down are you planning to dig?"

"All depends what we find along the way."

"Speaking of finding something, I'd better go find Henrietta. Make sure she hasn't got herself into a situation. The cliffs, you said?"

"That's where she was headed."

Damn fool woman, Braydon thought as he guided his horse in the direction of the cliffs, which he knew to be a lot farther away than they looked. He also knew the solid-looking wall of rock was home to a series of caves, some of which wound underground for miles. He hoped Henrietta wasn't foolish enough to go exploring on her own and get lost.

His fears escalated when he came across her horse tethered in the one sketchy patch of shade. He tied his mount next to hers. The two horses were practically old friends now.

Damn woman could be anywhere! He put his hands around his mouth like a megaphone he'd seen outside the circus when it was in Yuma. "Henrietta!"

His voice echoed back, bouncing off the rock cliffs like a mocking imitation of himself. In the distance he saw several birds startle and take to flight from where they had nested in the craggy outcroppings. He waited till the echo died down then tried again, projecting his voice in a different direction this time. After a third fruitless try he started toward the mouth of one of the larger caves when Henrietta came scampering into sight.

"Lord-a-mercy," she said, "I'm right here. No need to be making enough noise to wake the dead."

"You shouldn't be out here alone," he said. "And you sure as hell shouldn't be trooping through those caves alone. Real easy to get lost."

"Why, Braydon Mason." She swayed toward him with a saucy little wiggle of her hips. "Keep that up, and a girl might get the idea you care what happens to her."

He pressed his lips together. Henrietta was a heck of a lot easier to handle when the two of them were sparring and trading insults than when she came on all sweet as one of Georgina's gooey desserts in her cafe.

"Percy knows where I am."

"Percy *thinks* he knows where you are. Be a whole different game if darkness fell and you weren't back at the camp."

She tilted up her head toward him in a way that made him want to kiss her and spank her at the same time. He felt the front of his pants grow tight at the thought of her cute little butt, all naked and—

"Don't you want to know what I found?"

"You tell me. Do I want to know?"

"Seeing as how this is Copper Moon land, I should think you'd want to know. Not only did I see someone over here the other day, whoever it was was trespassing. Scraping around for mineral samples far as I can tell."

"What do you know about mineral sampling?"

"I wager I know a lot more than you do."

She had him there. Doubtless all sorts of things she knew more about. He wasn't sure he liked that. Usually he was the one with more life experiences than the ladies.

Henrietta was different. In so many ways. He stared at her deliciously full red lips, remembering how they'd felt under his. "We're a long way from the Dakota gold rush. A tad far-fetched to think there's gold in these here hills."

"Say what you like. It's clear someone believes there's something here of value. I saw recent marks that look like they'd been made by an assayer. Could help explain why Hawkes has been so hell-bent determined to get his hands on the ranch."

"Who told you that?"

"Laura. She said it's been going on as long as Hawkes has been here, going back to Brody's uncle's time. Said Hawkes was on the verge of bankrupting the old man when Brody showed up. One more reason Hawkes hates Brody and everything he stands for."

Braydon didn't want to talk about Hawkes. Not until the man was no longer a threat to Bullet and everyone who lived here. "At any rate, you told me you were ready to put me to work, so here I am."

"Yes, indeed," Henrietta said, with a smug little smile. "Here you are."

～

"THANK GOODNESS YOU'RE BACK," Laura said to Amanda. She'd been hanging near their cabin, not wanting to disturb the happy couple, but dying to catch up with her friend. "Can you hitch up the buggy? I need to get off this ranch before I go mad."

Amanda gave her a hug. "Nice to know someone missed me. Where we off to?"

"I need to see Georgina. We need to talk about the dance hall."

"I thought you said you didn't want to be involved anymore. On account of your condition and all."

"I only told Bradley that so he'd step up and help you."

"Matchmaking, were we?" Amanda said.

Laura found something terribly interesting on the ground near her feet. "Maybe just a little."

"Shouldn't you tell Brody where we're going?"

"I left him a note. That way he can't try to stop us. He's been fit to be tied ever since someone snatched up Henrietta and Percy. Barely lets me out of his sight."

"Wait! What about Henrietta and Percy?"

Laura swung herself into the buggy next to her friend. "It was nothing serious. Drifters looking for an easy victim. Likely long gone by now."

Amanda barked out a laugh. "I don't see Henrietta being easy or a victim."

Laura glanced over her shoulder. "Let's get going before Brody sees us and tries to stop us."

"Not much going on in Bullet," Amanda said as they reached town and drove down Main Street.

"Another reason we need to get started on plans for the dance hall. Give the townsfolk something to get excited about."

"Stop at the café first?" Amanda asked.

"Indeed. I'm dying for a nice glass of Georgina's sweet iced tea."

"Oh, look at that wagon over there. That's the travelling library I told you about. Where I borrowed those books you're reading. I wonder where Storm is. I'd love for you to meet her."

"Me too. She sounds fascinating."

Laura waited while Amanda secured their buggy. Inside the café, Georgina met them with an enthusiastic hug.

"Just the ladies I was hoping to see. I have someone here I want you to meet."

"Storm," Amanda said with a squeal. "I just saw the wagon outside. This is my good friend Laura. I was just telling her all about you."

Laura knew in an instant she was going to like the quiet, brown-haired beauty who was seated in a booth at the back of the café.

"You must be the schoolteacher. Pleasure to meet you. I was telling Amanda that driving from town to town is not quite as glamorous as it sounds, but it's most rewarding."

"So many folks out this way have no access to books. What you're doing is wonderful."

"We were just talking about women in business," Georgina said, "and the way I expanded the café last year."

Storm's grey eyes sparkled. "I don't get out this way very often, so I suggested to Georgina that maybe she could start a small lending library in the café."

"Where would the books come from?" Laura leaned forward in rapt attention. This is what she had missed being holed up at the ranch.

"A lot of them get donated. People move and can't take all their belongings. Sometimes we have a patron who orders books from the east." Storm spread her hands wide on the table. "There are so many adults who never learned to read. You'd find it rewarding to offer them an environment where they could learn."

"Now you're talking about something bigger than a book nook at the back of the café."

"I guess I am," Storm said with a smile. "Just trying to make folks lives better, one book at a time."

Laura gave Amanda's foot a subtle kick under the table. "Think if we had some sort of community-type hall built here in town. That could be a spot for a reading group and library."

"Are there plans for one?" Storm asked.

Laura shot Amanda a look. "There might be." She turned back to Storm. "A while back I came across someone who is word-blind. Smart as a whip but can't make hide nor hair out of letters or numbers."

"I've managed to help a few folks with that," Storm said.

"How?" Laura asked.

"Well, I write with the wrong hand from most folks. So when I was younger it made more sense to read and write backwards. I had to train myself the other way."

"So you might be able to help my ... my friend," Laura said. "I feel bad because even though I'm a teacher, I couldn't help him."

"I can show you a few easy steps to get started, at least," Storm said.

"That would be wonderful."

Laura returned home, immensely cheered by their little outing to town. Her jubilation was short-lived. Brody was waiting for them when they reached the ranch. One look at his face, and Laura knew something was wrong.

"I was just about to come looking for you," he said as he lifted her down from the buggy. "Don't you be taking off like that again, you hear?"

"What is it? What's wrong?" Laura asked.

"Blake found a bunch of dead rats near the well. Looks like someone is trying to poison us."

CHAPTER 6

"More water, Braydon?" Henrietta was sifting through the latest bag of sand Braydon had dumped near her feet an hour ago. The dig site had grown every day, thanks largely to Braydon's efforts. Percy wasn't much use behind a shovel. He was better off following up on anything Henrietta tagged from the site that might be of interest.

"Love some, thanks." Braydon straightened and wiped a sheen of perspiration from his forehead. He'd been working shirtless all day, and Henrietta was doing her best not to notice the way sunlight sheened the contours of his perspiration-dampened muscles. Did those muscles get bigger every day, or was she just noticing them more?

He vaulted out of the knee-deep dig and came toward her. She passed him a canteen, making sure her fingers brushed his as she did so. He pushed back his hat and his dark hair looked even darker, damp with perspiration from his efforts in the heat.

"You've been in the sun a long time," she said. "Maybe you should take a break."

His Adam's apple bobbed as he drank deeply. Lowering the canteen, he locked eyes with her as he swiped the back of his hand across his mouth. Henrietta's gaze slid past his eyes to where several droplets of water clung to two days' worth of sexy dark stubble shadowing his jawline.

"I'll take a break if you will." He stood before her, big and strong and capable. He tipped back his hat, and her gaze riveted to his chest, where a V-shaped smattering of dark hair emphasized his masculine build before it thinned to a single dark line that disappeared into his trousers.

She took a deep breath, which proved to be a mistake. All she could smell was Braydon. All musky, sun-warmed male, underscored by leather.

He'd worked tirelessly these past few days, staying until well after dark and arriving in the morning, just as she and Percy started to stir. It felt like the more she oohed and aahed over every little thing Braydon did around the dig site, the harder he worked to impress her with his prowess and abilities. Trouble was, it was working. She looked forward to the time they spent together each day, happy to leave Percy behind at camp, bent over his research papers and numerical formulas.

"What are you up to, Hen?" Percy asked, after Braydon's first day at the camp. "I've never seen you act like a drooling idiot over a man before."

"Catching flies with honey. And he's falling for it," Henrietta said. "He really thinks he has me on the line and just has to reel me in."

"I'm regretting I ever told you about the wager," Percy said. "He's really not a bad guy."

"Maybe not, if you take away his over-inflated ego," Henrietta said. "I doubt Braydon's ever had a woman turn him down before. And never in front of his entire family."

"Just remember. Any time you stick your hand in the fire, you're bound to get burned," Percy said.

"Because you know so much about women," Henrietta scoffed.

"You'd be surprised what I know," Percy said, with a mysterious smile she had never seen before. Just what secrets was her friend keeping to himself?

～

"Wish I could help you a few more days longer," Braydon said as he dragged an old blanket under the one sickly, desert ironwood tree. "But Brody's going to need me back at the ranch any time now. The others are due back with the new herd."

"Did you tell Brody about the markings I saw in the cave?"

"I did." Braydon shrugged. "He didn't set much store in it. Dismissed it as more than likely ancient cave drawings by some early natives in this area. Told me to ask you not to say anything about it."

Henrietta knew for certain that what she'd seen was not ancient drawings. But why should she care who was trespassing on ranch land if Brody didn't?

Once they were seated in the dappled shade, Braydon leaned back on his elbows, long legs stretched out in front of him. It was an inviting pose, as if he was asking her to join him. She reached out and touched a puckered scar on one shoulder. "What happened here?"

"Managed to stop a knife blade that was headed for my belly."

She raised a brow. "I didn't think you were the brawler in the family."

"I was forced to defend a certain lady's' dubious honor. Didn't go over well with the gentleman insulting her." He smoothly changed the subject. "What happens next once you find what you're looking for out here?"

"Evidence of Juan de Iturbe's ship? I expect we'll need to bring in a work crew and guards. That's when things get trickier. Before long, word will get out and we'll be besieged by fortune hunters from all over. Private land or not, it never seems to stop them."

Braydon was quiet for a good long time, so long she thought she must be boring him. "What if you don't bring in a work crew? What if my brothers and I came to work for you instead? No one in town would even have to know about the find."

"Why would you and your brothers do that?"

"We don't want the ranch overrun any more than you do. I'm actually surprised Percy talked Brody into agreeing to allow you two out here in the first place."

"Percy can be most convincing."

He gave her a look she was coming to know well. A look that promised to unearth all her deepest secrets. "Something tells me he's not the only one."

As he spoke, Braydon tugged her support arm so she toppled onto her side, facing him. Not that she put up much of a protest. She'd been waiting for his next move, and patience had never been her long suit. But it had to seem as if the two of them getting closer was all his idea.

He reached up and removed her wide-brimmed hat, tossing it to the ground behind them, along with his. Then he tangled his fingers through her hair before he brushed the curve of her jawline with the backs of his fingers. Her scalp tingled from his touch, shooting heated darts of awareness through her. She moved her head just enough to trap his hand between her face and her collarbone.

He responded by stroking the soft skin of her neck. Now those damn little arrows from his touch were ricocheting off her collarbone and skimming her bosom. She was acutely aware of her feminine curves, a swelling of her bosom and a tightening of her nipples beneath her chemise and white blouse.

She was worried he might notice her body's response, but luckily his eyes remained glued to hers as he trailed one hand over her ribs to seek out the indentation of her waist and the curve of her hips. She caught her breath, afraid her slightest move might signal that his touch was unwelcome.

Instead, she placed one hand, flat-palmed, against the smooth skin of his chest. She could feel the steady beat of his heart beneath her fingertips.

He caught her hand in his. "Do I have any reason to be worried about you alone out here with Percy once I leave for the day?"

He frowned when she laughed to hide a crow of triumph. Clearly, her ploy was working if he was making noise about being jealous of Percy.

"Well, it is unconventional, you know. An unmarried woman and man traveling the world together, unchaperoned and all."

She batted her lashes in what she hoped was a flirtatious way and didn't just look like she had something in her eye. "Braydon Mason. Am I to believe you've never spent time alone with a woman in all your years?"

A muscle jumped in his jaw. "I didn't say that."

"Let me assure you, Percy is really not my type. Even though he's a very wonderful friend." She pressed her lips together. "A much better friend than any of my brothers."

"I have no interest in being your friend, Henny."

"No?" She tilted her head. "What did you have in mind?"

"Kissing you, for starters."

"Do you think we need a chaperone?"

"Why ruin the fun?"

His kiss this time was more magical than last, masterful and skilled in the way his lips shaped hers beneath them. She felt everything inside her respond with a soft shifting, a gentle flow, as she relaxed back and wrapped her arms around his neck, urging him closer.

He needed no other encouragement, his lips only leaving hers to plunder secret spots like behind her ear, before flicking her lobe with his tongue and causing her to shiver in excitement. The sensitive skin below her ear that stretched to her jaw and neck was explored in great thoroughness as he licked and nibbled.

She felt his hand glide over her hips and ribs to lightly graze the underside of her breast and, much as she welcomed his touch, she couldn't appear too eager. Gently she laced her fingers through his roving hand, in a move designed to signal "not now", but perhaps at some future date.

Braydon returned to a somber bunch at the Copper Moon, grim-faced around the big table in the main ranch house kitchen. The ladies were nowhere in sight, which meant this was serious.

He took the chair next to Bradley and dug an elbow into that man's ribs. "Was the wedding night that bad? I did offer to give you some advice, you might recall."

Bradley gave him a long, assessing glance. "If you're half

the ladies' man you claim to be, what's with the wager that you can win Miss Henrietta over to your womanizing way?"

Braydon tipped his chair back and propped one booted foot onto the table top, giving his nails a pretend buff on his shirt front. "Already planning how to spend my winnings. That gal is all but eating out of my hand."

"Long as she's not drinking out of our well," Brody said.

Braydon swung his leg down and spun around on his seat. "What's with the well?"

"You know the one out front?" Brody said.

"The old one from back in your uncle's day that dried out years ago?"

"It would seem there was enough water in it to poison some rats hanging around. And whoever was responsible for contaminating it didn't know that it wasn't our water source."

Braydon let out a low whistle. "Arsenic always was Hawkes's poison of choice."

Brody pinched the skin between his eyebrows as if a headache was brewing. "I just don't know when someone could have got close in here. You haven't been around much lately, but the rest of us have. We've been keeping an extra-close watch in case of something like this."

"It must have happened when we were at the wedding," Blake said. "That's the only time no one was here at the ranch."

"Henrietta was pretty certain she spotted someone out near the cliffs last week," Braydon said.

"That's a long way away from the well," Brody said.

"Didn't her and Percy say they thought the thugs that jumped them the night of the wedding came from the direction of the ranch?" Blake said.

"They did," Braydon said shortly. The thought of some

thug with his hands on Henrietta made his blood boil. He glanced over at Brody. "You worried about the others making it back safely?"

"I always worry about the family."

"What if they also got to the second well?" Braydon said. "Wouldn't there have been symptoms before now?"

"Bradley's taking a sample to Yuma tomorrow. Get his buddy to check it out for us. In the meantime, we spent most of the day hauling water from the river. Don't drink anything that hasn't been boiled first. Just to be on the safe side."

Braydon stood. "Anyone know what happened to that beer keg we brought back from the wedding? I don't know about the rest of you, but I could sure use a pint right about now."

"Is working your way into Henrietta's heart making you thirsty?" Bradley asked.

"Knowing Braydon, it's more like her knickers he's working his way into," said Blake.

"Gentlemen don't kiss and tell," Braydon said with a smug smile. "Soon as the others get back, I'll invite Henrietta over here for a family dinner. That way, you all can see firsthand just how irresistible she finds me."

HAWKES PULLED up at the assigned meeting place outside of town, away from prying eyes and flapping ears. He didn't trust these men he'd hired, aware they'd happily stick a knife through his ribs the second he turned his back if there was anything in it for them.

The sheriff had recruited the gang, and good help was hard to find. With Don Lucas breathing down his neck, demanding results in their joint mining venture, and cutting him off from any more funds ... Hawkes grew thirsty just thinking about it. His creditors were circling around like buzzards, ready to jump his carcass at the first sign of weakness.

The old days of holding up another stagecoach any time funds grew short were no more, so he was forced to keep borrowing.

His thirst grew, and he patted his vest pocket to make sure his trusty flask was near at hand. "I thought you all said the deed was done."

"Just like you said," their ringleader answered. He was an ugly brute with a jagged scar down one cheek. "T'other night when everyone was in town."

"No one saw you near the well?"

"Nah!"

"So why haven't I heard that any of them are taking ill?"

The second-in-command spat a thin stream of tobacco juice onto the ground near Hawkes. "Takes time for the arsenic to work. How long before your old lady up and croaked?"

"I was found not guilty of that charge."

The four men laughed.

"Doesn't mean you didn't do it," the leader said.

Hawkes glowered. Killing his wife had felt good at the time, getting even with her for passing that bastard off as his. If he'd known the generous allowance from her family would die when she did, he might have kept her alive.

Hell with it. He pulled out his flask and took a deep swallow. Instantly he felt better. His hands felt steadier.

"You sure you don't want us to take care of the other two? That foppish dandy and the gal who wears them men's clothes?"

"Not right now. Maybe at some point." For now, Hawkes was holding out hope Sir Percy would find that fool ship of pearls he was looking for. Big cache of pearls would take care of his financial woes and then some.

The big, burly dude of the four pulled out a wicked curved blade and proceeded to pick his teeth with it. "Let us know. Got me a hankering for some sweet foreign meat."

Hawkes didn't know if the thug meant Percy or Henrietta, and quite frankly, he didn't care.

THE SECOND HENRIETTA heard the sound of a horse and rider approaching the dig site, she reached for her gun, and only put it back down when she recognized Braydon. She hadn't seen him for a few days and had no intention of admitting that she had missed him. She'd been enjoying herself way too much in their little game of advance, retreat, advance, then fall back.

She stood as he got close, tossed her head and stuck her chest out. "I thought maybe you'd forgotten about me," she said in her most flirty tone.

He dismounted and covered the ground between them in three long strides. "I'm pretty sure you know that's not possible."

She looked up at him, lashes fluttering. "A girl never knows for sure."

"Count on it." He scooped her up and held her aloft so she was looking down at him. He spun her in a circle, his hands firm on her waist. "Your pretty face is the last thing I think of at night and the first thing I think about when I wake."

She tried to wiggle free. "Braydon Mason. Why do I have cause to doubt your sincerity?"

He placed her gently back on her feet, and pretended to sulk. "Now my feelings are hurt."

"You're hurt?" She tilted her head teasingly. "Perhaps you want for me to kiss it better?"

"Hell, yeah!" He caught her against him so tight she could barely breathe. She could feel him intimately at every juncture their bodies met. Hardened thigh muscles pressed against her legs. His hips met hers in such a way she couldn't resist sliding her hands around his waist and touching his leather belt as his hard-muscled chest molded her soft contours.

He deliberately ground his hips against hers, and she felt the stab of his belt buckle against her stomach. Except it wasn't his belt.

Last time she'd been held this close against a man, she'd been a terrified teenager. As a mature woman, she was finding it an altogether different experience. Not frightening at all. On the contrary, her skin flushed and tingled, making her hot and needy and achy all over.

The tiniest shift on her part, and her nipples swooned from the resultant pressure, needing, wanting more. A pleasant sensation radiated through her. She felt every bone and muscle in her body grow soft and pliant in an effort to better fit against Braydon.

"Maybe this wasn't such a good idea," he said, his warm breath fanning her eagerly waiting lips. "You've got me aching a dozen different ways to Sunday."

She tilted her head provocatively. "And if I told you you weren't the only one?"

"I'd say you're unlike any woman I've ever met before."

"You want me to act different?"

"Not for one bronco-bucking second."

He kissed her then, hard and possessive. His lips branded hers before his mouth softened, persuasively coaxing her lips to open, to grant him access.

She linked her hands behind his neck, locking him in place as she pulled out a few moves of her own. She might not have been kissed very much or very often, but she was an avid reader. In her travels, she'd discovered and devoured several books her mother would consider improper reading for a lady. Only a few years earlier, *Kama Sutra* had been published in English, and even though she knew it had been somewhat modified from the original version, she still found it fascinating reading.

How generous of Braydon to afford her the opportunity to put some of her research into practice.

She heard his breath catch as she took over the role of aggressor. Her tongue mated with his, demanding more. She made little mewling noises in the back of her throat like a hungry kitten, before she bit his bottom lip. Hard enough for him to know it was deliberate, not hard enough to draw blood. Immediately, she pulled it into her mouth and soothed it, as if in apology.

She felt the rigid hardness of him swell against her stomach, and rolled her hips encouragingly from side to side. Her nipples were hard pebbles of want, seeking, needing the brush of his fingertips through the thin cotton of her blouse.

She placed her hands on his chest finding the ridge of hard, masculine nipples beneath his shirt, in a deliberate invitation for him to do the same. She glanced up to see the way his eyes darkened as his pupils dilated, and his hands cupped the rounded softness of her breasts.

She swayed toward him on weakened legs, unprepared

for the rush of heated desire flooding her nether regions at his touch. She caught her breath and took a deliberate step back, aware of the puzzled way he was watching her. She had surprised him which was good.

She had also surprised herself, which was not good.

She liked to be in control of all aspects of herself and her life. To have Braydon ignite certain foreign desires in her hadn't been part of the bargain. But she recovered quickly, fanning herself with one hand and making light of her response.

"My, my," she said, in a forced Southern-belle accent she had heard once and liked to practice from time to time. "You do turn a girl's head, Braydon Mason."

"You're a bit of a distraction yourself," he said, worrying his lower lip as if still feeling the pull of her gentle bite. "I almost forgot why I came out here."

"Oh." She fluttered her lashes again. "Not just to see little old me?"

"Besides that." He straightened his shoulders as if fighting for control of a situation that had somehow gotten away from him. "I came to invite you for supper at the ranch tomorrow. And Percy of course. The boys are back from Mexico with the new herd so we're having a little celebration."

"I can't speak for Percy. But as for me, I'd love that. It will be a pleasure to spend more time with your family."

That puzzled frown was back on his handsome face. The one that told her he was finding her more than a bit of an enigma, and it both frustrated and intrigued him.

She sashayed to his side and pressed a quick kiss to his lips. "I need to get back to work now. You've distracted me enough for one day."

CHAPTER 7

"I'll stop by at the camp on my way out and invite Percy to supper."

"You do that." She was unable to stop her gaze from following him as he swung into the saddle and turned his horse around. Damn if those trousers he wore didn't pull across his derriere in a most pleasing way. Some new-fangled breeches created by a Mr. Levi. Trust Braydon to be in the latest fashion.

She hadn't been back to work more than a few minutes before she once more heard the pounding of horse hooves coming her way. Didn't anyone want her to get any work done today? She grabbed her rifle, appreciating its weight in her hand, only to put it down when she recognized Braydon.

"Henny, come quick. Something's wrong with Percy."

She clambered out of the site and raced for her horse. By the time she was mounted, Braydon was well in the lead and she urged her horse faster, fear clutching at her heart.

Percy was her best friend, her colleague, the one person who had encouraged her to be and act exactly as she chose. She'd never before considered the danger involved in what they did, not even when they had been overtaken by those ruffians the other night. An encounter like that could happen to anyone, anywhere in the world.

At the base camp, she reined in her horse and was out of the saddle before it had fully come to a stop, running and catching her balance at the same time. Braydon was there ahead of her, elevating Percy's head and examining a red spot on his neck. He looked up at her with concern.

"He's got a fever. I'm no expert, but this looks like a spider bite on his neck. The black widow is venomous if that's what caused it. He'll need to see a doctor."

"Let's not waste time talking about it," Henrietta said. "Let's get him to town."

Percy waved a hand through the air. "Can't have a fever. Too cold. Damnation, everything hurts."

Henrietta knelt at his side, aware his breathing sounded labored, as if he was having trouble taking in enough air. "What hurts?"

"All of it. My chest. My gut. My lungs."

"Can you ride?"

"Of course I can ride." She exchanged a glance with Braydon. Percy's speech was labored.

"I seriously doubt that, my friend. Come on." Braydon hauled Percy to his feet, ducked underneath one shoulder to take most of Percy's weight and slowly made his way to his waiting horse. "I'll get him on. You make sure he doesn't slip back off while I mount."

Henrietta worried her bottom lip and did as he said, stabilizing Percy's weight on the front of the saddle while Braydon mounted up behind the injured man.

She was shocked to realize how grateful she was for Braydon's presence. Heaven only knew what she would have done if she'd been on her own and found Percy.

Don't be a ninny. She would have coped, she told herself, as she mounted up and followed Braydon's horse. She was more than capable. She'd never needed a man before, and wasn't about to start now.

It seemed forever before they reached Bullet and the office of Doc Parsons.

"How do, Braydon. Whatcha got for me this time? One of the brothers get himself in a bit of a situation?"

"Not this time, doc. Percy's got a puncture wound on his neck. Could be from a black widow."

"Well, bring him through. You know the routine."

"Are you some sort of regular here?" Henrietta hissed, as she took Percy's other side and helped maneuver his limp form into the doctor's back room.

Braydon didn't answer.

"Hmmm," the doctor said, after Braydon managed to place Percy on his examination table. "Black widows don't usually attack folks unless provoked."

"Having a nap," Percy mumbled.

The doctor turned Percy's head to examine the bright red swollen area on his neck. From there, he placed his stethoscope against Percy's chest.

The doctor turned to her as if seeing her for the first time. "Fetch me some ice from the ice-box, would you, girlie?"

Henrietta gritted her teeth at being called "girlie". She doubted the doctor would have ordered Braydon around as if he was an indentured servant. Still, she hustled to do his bidding. Anything to help Percy.

It took her a few minutes to find the ice-box and longer still to break off a decent-size chunk with the ice pick.

"About time," was all the doctor said upon her return. Then he turned to address Braydon, as if Henrietta wasn't even in the room. "Ice will help take the swelling down and relieve the pain from the bite. Don't let him eat anything till this evening. It's bound to make him nauseous."

"What about the fever and the headache?" Braydon asked.

"It'll pass. Hard to say when. Every spider injects a different amount of venom. For now, see that he gets lots of rest. Plenty of water ought to help sweat out the fever."

"'Kay, doc, thanks."

Henrietta stood stiffly, waiting to be noticed. "How much do we owe you, doctor?"

Once again, the doctor ignored her and addressed Braydon. "Have the gentleman come by when he's better. We can square up then. With any luck, he should be right as rain before long."

"Are all the men in Bullet like that?" Henrietta fumed, as they left the doctor's office and loaded Percy back onto Braydon's horse.

"Like what?" Braydon asked.

Henrietta blew out an exasperated breath as she mounted her horse and wheeled him toward the house Percy had rented as their headquarters. "Never mind."

One thing was for sure. It was going to be extremely satisfying to trounce Braydon on his ear in front of everyone.

"Are you sure you feel well enough to be up and about?" Henrietta asked Percy, the following day.

"Henny, for pity's sake, quit fussing over me. If I say I'm well enough to attend the Masons' supper party tonight, then I am quite well enough."

"Because I wouldn't mind staying home with you," she said. "If you're not up to it."

Percy paused in the midst of tying his cravat, and turned to study her. "Are you trying to use me as an excuse to avoid this evening?"

"Of course not. Why ever would you say that?"

"Don't forget how well I know you, my dear."

Drat Percy. He did know her through and through, secrets and all. Henrietta flipped through her frocks, trying to decide which one was suitable to openly reject and ridicule Braydon in front of his peers. He had already seen the green one that night she burned the roast and they went to Yuma.

Her movements slowed. He had been both charming and gentlemanly that evening, kind to those two older ladies of dubious reputation. And later, he displayed an unexpected vulnerability regarding his parentage and unorthodox upbringing. How odd it must feel to not know for certain who your mother is. To not have a real family.

Small wonder he was so fiercely loyal to the Mason clan. She expected each one of the boys had his own story about how he came to be part of the group calling the Copper Moon Ranch home.

In the end, she decided on the scarlet-colored gown because it reminded her of her mother. She wondered how her mother was, immersed in a life of domesticity Henrietta had turned her back on. Would her mother be proud of the woman Henrietta had become? Would she regret taking her husband's side and banishing her only daughter? For that matter, had it really been a banishment? Perhaps Madre was simply trying to give her daughter opportunities she herself had not had as a young woman.

She stepped into the gown and fastened the row of onyx

buttons up the front, pleased by the way the gown empha-sized the silhouette of her female shape, making her waist appear smaller and her bosom almost lush. The good thing about so rarely being seen in feminine attire was the added impact when she did dress like a lady.

She added some ruby earrings that had been her grand-mother's and highlighted her cheekbones with a rare touch of rouge. She pulled the front of her hair back and up in a casual, yet becoming look that left the back of her hair cascading over partially bare shoulders.

She took herself out to find Percy, where she performed a little twirl for his inspection.

He let out a low whistle. "Why do I get the feeling you're not only going to shred Braydon in front of everyone, you're also planning to stomp all over his heart in the bargain?"

She flipped open her fan in an exaggerated move. "That, my friend, is because you know me better than anyone else can hope to." She draped a light, shimmery shawl across her shoulders. She had bought it in Greece because it reminded her of the sun setting over the Mediterranean.

"Poor bastard," Percy said. "He may never recover."

"As long as I wound more than his pocketbook," Henri-etta said.

"I'm most certain of that."

Over her protest, Percy insisted on driving their rig out to the Copper Moon ranch. "I'm hardly an invalid, Hen."

"I didn't like seeing you hurt. The two of us have a lot more work here to accomplish."

Percy slanted her a look. "I feel like we're getting closer all the time."

They arrived at the ranch without incident. Light spilled from every window of the ranch house, and the open front door. They could hear boisterous laughter and raised voices even before they reached the walkway.

Clearly, Braydon had been watching for their arrival. He hurried out to help Henrietta alight. "I'm so happy you were able to join us this evening." He turned to Percy. "I take it you are feeling far better than yesterday."

"Indeed. I appreciate your help getting me to the doctor when you did."

"It was nothing." Braydon turned admiring eyes upon Henrietta. "You are absolutely breathtaking."

"Thank you." Henrietta slipped her hand through his bent elbow, thinking they'd come a long way from him telling her she cleaned up good when they were at the wedding.

"How are the newlyweds?" she asked.

"Come see for yourself."

Inside the ranch house, Braydon whisked her shawl from her shoulders and hung it just inside the door. The table, set for eleven, looked bigger than she recalled. She paused on the threshold of the room, overcome by memories of home, where their dinner table had been set for twelve. She might be in a different part of the world, but families everywhere were still families, gathering together to share a meal and talk about their day.

Except she wasn't family. And she didn't really belong here. Not the way Laura and Amanda did. The thought vanished as she was enfolded in hugs by both women. But she still felt like a fraud, an interloper. She was only here because of some stupid bet Braydon had made with his brothers. He didn't really like her or care about her. A fact she'd do well to remember.

"It's wonderful to have you here, Henrietta." Laura said.

"Yes," Amanda agreed. "You must tell us all about what's

happening out at the camp. I understand Braydon has been out there most days lately."

"He's been a wonderful help," Henrietta said. "I don't know what I would have done without him when Percy was feverish and ill from that spider bite yesterday."

"He looks quite recovered."

"Strong constitution, I expect," Henrietta said. She smiled at Laura. "Brody must be relieved to have everyone back safe and sound."

"We all are." Amanda took her arm. "Have you met all my brothers-in-law?"

"Only a few," Henrietta admitted. "I confess I haven't quite got them properly sorted out."

Amanda laughed. "That takes some time. And don't expect to ever sort out the twins. Just when you think you've got it figured out, they'll turn the tables and pretend to be each other."

"That must be most confusing for the ladies," Henrietta said.

"They do it deliberately," Amanda said. "Barron, Bishop. Come say hello to Miss Henrietta."

Henrietta was daunted that, up close, the two young men were the mirror-image of each other. "Welcome back," she said. "I gather you had a fruitful trip south."

"Yes ma'am," the one she thought might be Bishop, answered.

She cringed slightly at the address. "Please call me Henrietta."

"Yes, ma'am. I mean Henrietta."

The other one chimed in. "Bishop and I took turns confusing the seller so bad, he didn't know if he was coming or going."

"Got an extra twenty head out of the deal," Bishop said.

"You boys are terrible," Laura said. "One of these days your conning ways will catch up with you with devastating results."

Brody approached and laid a loving arm around his wife. "Well, my sweet. Just think of it as them both being shrewd negotiators. Seller beware."

"And ladies beware," Amanda chimed in before she moved away, pulling Henrietta along with her. "That takes care of Brody and Bradley and the twins. The other two rascals are Benjamin over in the far corner and Blake talking to Braydon. Blake was the first one Braydon took under his wing. He's the one Laura fusses over because letters and numbers make no sense to him. She's hoping our new friend Storm might be able to help him. Despite not being able to read or write, he's brilliant with anything mechanical, and Brody relies heavily on him around the ranch. Benjamin is a little on the shy side but a skilled marksman. I always feel better knowing he's traveling with the others when they're away."

"I certainly appreciate the update," Henrietta said. "I come from a family with nine older brothers, so I understand about the different personalities."

"Yes, they don't always get along this well. But they have oodles of respect for Brody, and he calls the shots."

Henrietta sensed Braydon's presence behind her, even before he pressed against her in a possessive gesture and insinuated himself between her and Amanda. "You're monopolizing my date, Amanda, and ignoring that poor dude you recently married."

Amanda raised a questioning brow, her gaze sliding from Braydon to Henrietta and back to Braydon. "So that's the way of things, is it?"

"We've spent some enjoyable time together," Braydon

said smoothly before Henrietta could find her voice. "I thought it was time she meets the rest of the clan."

Amanda patted Henrietta's shoulder. "I'll do you a favor and warn you right now. Despite his reputation as a ladies' man, Braydon is an honorable man. Isn't that right, Braydon?"

Henrietta straightened. Was that an underlying warning in Amanda's tone to Braydon? Perhaps she also knew of the wager and disapproved.

Henrietta swallowed and turned toward Braydon with what she hoped was an openly admiring glance. "I'm quite certain Braydon is not one to trifle with a lady's feelings. He's always behaved in a most appropriate fashion when we are together."

Amanda gave Braydon a warning poke in the chest with her finger. "I expect to hear things stay that way."

Braydon gave his head a rueful shake as Amanda glided through the crowd and began herding the others in the direction of the table. "I had a slew of mothering growing up. Never had a sister until just recent." He took her arm. "We'd best go take our seats before she really gets bossy."

At the meal's end, Henrietta rose to help clear but was effectively shooed back to her seat by Braydon. "You're our guest," he said and surprised her by lifting her plate, along with his own and Percy's, and carrying them to the sink. In her family, not one of the men would have considered lifting a plate from the table to the sink if his life depended on it.

Across from her, Brody kept a watchful eye on his wife, Laura. He leaned in close to her and spoke in tones so soft and caring, Henrietta almost felt guilty of eavesdropping.

"Tired, my sweet?" One hand rested lightly on Laura's shoulder.

"A little," she said. "Isn't it wonderful to have everyone back, safe and sound and all together?"

"Almost as wonderful as knowing our young one is on his or her way to join the family," Brody said, his big hand resting lightly on Laura's stomach.

Henrietta swallowed thickly, never before having witnessed this type of loving interaction between a husband and wife. Her father had barely spoken to her mother except to bark orders. And never with such a loving tone of voice.

Braydon returned to the table with two cups of coffee and settled back next to her. In a seemingly casual gesture, he rested a proprietary arm across the back of her chair, allowing his fingers to graze the exposed skin of her shoulder. From there she felt him begin to softly stroke her hair, twining a strand between two fingers in a way that spoke to his right to touch her in so intimate a fashion.

"These are pretty."

Shivers ran through her as he stroked her ear, using her earrings as an excuse to touch her even more intimately. "Thank you. They belonged to my grandmother."

"Lucky you." Was that a wistful tone in his voice? "To not only know who your grandmother is but to be able to spend time with her."

"I lived with her in England for several years until she passed. She was years ahead of her time. She encouraged me to go to Oxford, which is where Percy and I met."

"I didn't know women could attend university."

"Times are changing. Even though women can't receive a degree, they are permitted to sit in on the classes."

He gave her an indulgent smile. "That helps to explain a lot. About who you are, I mean."

Henrietta pressed her lips together. She hadn't intended

to share so much with Braydon, but somehow, he had a knack for drawing it out of her.

Subtly, she took a sip of coffee as she studied the others around the table. There was no mistaking the keen way several of the brothers were watching her and Braydon. Were they waiting for more? How thick was he planning to lay it on in order to claim his mastery over the female sex and claim his winnings?

CHAPTER 8

H awkes all but fell off his horse as the mount came to a jerky stop in front of Madam Zara's place in Yuma. Unsteadily, he wove his way up the front steps and hammered on the door. The peephole opened.

"Lemme in," he bellowed.

"Keep your voice down," Zara said, as she closed the peephole. He waited impatiently as he heard the bolts slide before the door finally opened. Hawkes pushed past her and scanned the front parlor. Couple of fancy dudes he'd not seen before. There was a new gal playing the piano. A tad skinny for his tastes but young and dumb, the way he liked them.

"Tell Dolly I'm here," he growled.

"Not until you hand over your gun. You know the rules," Zara said. Hawkes studied the slut through narrowed eyes. Zara had always talked down to him. She was getting older and uglier by the day, and he'd love to smash in her face with the butt of his revolver. Instead he passed the Colt over to her without comment.

"I'm afraid Dolly is all tied up at the moment," Zara said in haughty tones.

Hawkes growled his displeasure. What the hell! Just when a man was in need of a little female reassurance and attention. After all, he'd bankrolled the slut's latest stage flop. She was supposed to be at his beck and call.

"We didn't know to expect you," Zara said smoothly. "Perhaps one of the other girls would interest you."

"I'll wait." Dolly was the only one who knew the special treatment he required and exactly how administer it.

"Cash up front," Zara said.

"What's the matter? My credit no good?" His voice got as ugly as he could make it. "Don't forget who helped you buy this shit-hole in the first place."

Zara crossed her arms over her saggy boobs. "Our business arrangement ended years ago. As far as I'm concerned, you have used up all your credit. You don't run any charities, and neither do I."

Hawkes wiped the spittle from the corner of his mouth and tried to hang onto his fraying temper. He'd show this bitch! From the corner of his eye he saw a big, burly black guy closing in, just waiting for a sign from Zara. She passed the man Hawkes's gun.

"Mr. Hawkes was just leaving," Zara said to her lackey. "Kindly show him the way out."

Hawkes glared at her over his shoulder. "You just wait," he said, waving one fist in the air before he turned and stumbled over the door sill. He lurched onto the porch where he tried and failed to catch his balance before he hit the stairs. He toppled down, landing hard in the dust at the bottom.

The black bastard just stood and watched him. Laughing, Hawkes was certain.

"Don't just stand there!" he bellowed. "Help me up."

"I suggest you help yourself," the man said disdainfully. He disappeared inside before Hawkes lumbered to his feet.

Damn impertinent darky. Who the hell did he think he was?

Hawkes stopped in the saloon for a necessary shot of refreshment before he made the return trip. The saloon was noisy and crowded and he was jostled more than once as he shouldered his way to the bar.

Damn riff raff. They ought to have parted ranks and made way. Didn't they know who he was?

He wrapped his fist around his glass with a scowl. He ought to have been upstairs at Zara's right now, drinking her booze, pampered and safe with someone who understood him.

He was well on his way back to Bullet before he noticed he didn't have his gun.

BRODY WAS first to stand from the dinner table after their evening meal. "It's time Laura and I say our good nights." His gaze touched each Mason brother briefly. "Good to have everyone safely back and together."

Laura joined her husband, and Percy shot to his feet. "Many thanks to you all for the fine meal."

"You're very welcome," Laura said with a smile. "It's a nice change to have company. We must do it again some time."

"Indeed," added Amanda, as she rose, also, and looked questioningly toward Bradley. "Are you coming?"

"In a minute," Bradley said. "Couple things to discuss with the boys first."

"Walk over with us," Laura said. Amanda nodded with one last puzzled look toward her new husband.

Amanda must be wondering what was keeping him from the marital bed, even for a few minutes, Henrietta thought. Bradley must be in on the boys' wager and needed to be here.

Percy turned her way as the door closed behind the first three to depart. "I believe that is our signal to saddle up as well, Hen."

"Goodness, yes," Henrietta said. "I'm sure everyone here has an early morning, as do we."

She rose, closely followed by Braydon who remained within kissing distance, both hands resting proprietarily on her waist. She could feel his warm touch clear through the fabric.

"Will you miss me tomorrow?" One finger beneath her chin, he tilted her head as if to kiss her in front of everyone.

Henrietta reached for the closest thing at hand, her half-empty coffee cup, and dashed it in his face. "I most certainly will not miss you pawing me the way you have been all through our meal. It was only to save our hosts embarrassment that I refrained from requesting my seat be moved."

He didn't say a word as he raised one hand to wipe the droplets of cold coffee from his face.

"And another thing. You may have been raised in a brothel, but you can't treat respectable women as if they were all for sale."

Shocked silence rang through the room as she swung about, snatched up her shawl, and took her leave, Percy on her heels. The door had barely closed behind them when she heard the outbreak of jeers and laughter from Braydon's kin.

She descended the steps and flounced into the buggy next to Percy. "I showed him, didn't I?"

"You did that, Hen. All that and more."

So why did her actions not bring about the rush of satisfaction she had expected?

Back in her room, Henrietta disrobed and flung the red dress into a crumpled heap in one corner. It seemed unlikely she'd ever wear it again. It would render too many unpleasant memories of Braydon. She pulled off her ruby earrings and dropped them onto a small doily atop the dresser, vowing to put them safely away tomorrow.

Tugging on her night-dress, she crawled beneath the covers where sleep eluded her. Over and over she kept replaying in her head that final scene with Braydon. She told herself her actions were to ensure she trounced him as thoroughly as possible in front of the others.

In truth, she was remembering the pleasantly possessively feel of his hands on her bare skin. The intimate way his eyes found hers as the evening wore on, as if the two of them were alone in a private world. And much, much more.

BRAYDON THREW himself into work around the ranch with a vengeance. Without a word, he'd passed over his share of the recent profits to be split among the others, who knew better than to say anything, let alone crow about their victory.

More than once the other night, during dinner, he'd wished that stupid wager had never been made. He had enjoyed Henrietta at his side, looking so breathtakingly beautiful. Her wit, her intelligence, her easy manner with his family had all sparked something new and unfamiliar inside him.

He was a bastard and an arrogant one at that. He didn't deserve so fine a lady at his side. What would a high-born, well-educated woman want with the likes of him? Born on the wrong side of the blanket, raised in a whore house where not even his own mother laid claim to him.

The negative thoughts swirled through him, festering to the point where he noticed how the others gave him a wide berth as they moved a mature herd to fresh pastures in order to fatten them up before they eventually drove them west.

"What's eating you?" Brody came up quietly beside him. "Because whatever it is, quit taking it out on that poor horse of yours, and anyone unlucky enough to be within spitting distance."

Braydon pulled up his horse. "You got complaints about my work, spit it out."

"It's not your work," Brody said. "It's your attitude. Ever since that night Percy and Henrietta were at the ranch for supper, you've been like a bear with a sore paw. What went on after Laura and I left?"

"Nothing," Braydon said shortly.

"You want to take some time and go back to their camp and help out," Brody said, "all you need to do is ask. We can manage here."

Braydon shook his head. "Got all the work I need right here on the ranch."

"Take the day off then," Brody said. "Get some perspective. I've got enough to worry about without adding you to the list."

"Fine!" Braydon touched his heels to his mount's flanks and wheeled abruptly in the direction of the ranch.

It hadn't been easy these past few evenings, witnessing the gentle affection between Brody and Bradley and their brides when they joined in for the evening meal. Damn, if women on a ranch didn't prove more bad luck than women on a ship!

It was well past midday by the time he'd cleaned up and made his way to Yuma. He went around to the back door of Zara's place, knowing all too well he'd find her in the kitchen with some of the others, drinking coffee and sharing stories.

Zara looked up as he entered. "Aren't you a little old to be coming in the back door the way you did when you were young?"

The half a dozen women with her took one look at him, grabbed their cups, and made their excuses to leave.

Zara gave him a rueful look. "Time was when all the ladies waited for you to come home from school and share stories about your day. Now they see you and they disappear."

"Why do you suppose that is?" He pulled out a wooden chair, swung it around and straddled it so his arms rested along the wooden back as he faced Zara. "Afraid they might unwittingly divulge a secret? Or one of them might admit to being my mother?"

Zara rose and helped herself to more coffee from a pot on the back of the stove. "So that's what this is about?" She scrutinized him closely. "You find yourself a girl?"

Braydon flinched. "Why would you say that?"

"Kinda makes sense. Always figured one day you'd have a mind to start your own family, and get mired-up in stuff you don't know. Like where you came from. Kind of thing a decent woman might want to know before she goes birthing young of her own."

"I have no lady in my life," Braydon said. "But I sure do have questions. Like why she never claimed me. Why the big secret?"

Zara continued to study him, as if gauging his mood. "I'm ready for the truth, Zara. More than ready."

"Yes, I guess you are." She rose and went to a nearby sideboard. She came back with a bottle of whiskey and two glasses. She poured a measure of whiskey into each one. Somehow, Braydon figured he was going to need it.

"Truth is, your mother wasn't one of us."

His jaw dropped. "But I always believed ... you always implied..."

"I know. We were protecting your dear mother. She hailed from a good family and came to us when she was in trouble."

Braydon pressed his lips in a thin line. None of this made sense. "What do you mean 'in trouble'?"

"She was a pretty thing. Men flocked to her like bees to honey. Lost her heart to one, someone she knew her folks wouldn't approve of. He was killed sudden-like. Her folks would have disowned her had they known the truth, so she pretended to go out east for a year. Instead, she came here and had you. She stayed on for a while after you were born. It was really hard for her to leave, but her mother wasn't well, and she was nothing if not a dutiful daughter.

"We were supposed to put you in the orphanage, but you were such a darling wee thing. By the time she left, we were, all of us, in love with you. Could hardly blame us for deciding to keep you. Orphanages were nasty, evil places. We knew we could do a better job of raising you ourselves. And when you were old enough to start asking questions, well the lie just sort of grew and stuck." Zara shrugged and stared into her now-empty whiskey glass.

"Did you ever hear from my mother again?"

"Yuma's not that big of a town. The likes of her never socialized with the likes of us. She didn't know you were still with us. Eventually she got married and had another child. I'd pass her on the street from time to time. Always saw a shadow in her eyes. Figured it was because of her giving you up."

Braydon stood. "Where is she? I need to see her."

Zara looked at him and slowly nodded before she drew a pencil and piece of paper toward her. She wrote something down, folded it and passed it to him.

Braydon unfolded it and looked at it. "What is this?"

"It's a map of the cemetery at the old church on the other side of town. Shows the plot where she's buried." She rose, reached into a canister on the sideboard and pulled out a revolver. "Do me a favor and get rid of this, will you?"

Braydon took the gun she passed him. "Why?"

"Belongs to Hawkes. I want nothing to do with anything that's his."

HENRIETTA COULD NOT FIGURE out what was going on with Percy. Not only was he staying at the house in town, pleading lingering headaches from the spider bite, he absolutely forbade her to go out to the camp by herself.

"I'm just not up to it yet, Hen. Give me another day or two till I'm fully recovered."

"You know what they say when you get thrown off a horse," she said.

"A near-lethal bite from a poisonous spider is hardly the same thing," he said huffily. "I could have died."

"Hardly," she said impatiently. "If you're not back in the

saddle tomorrow, I'm going out to camp, with you or without you. Sitting around is driving me bat-crazy."

"So do something," Percy said. "Go visit Miss Laura. Catch up on the local gossip."

"I can't go out to Copper Moon," Henrietta said. "Not after ... You know. What happened the other evening."

"Now you're acting like a goose. She wasn't even there when you emptied your cup of coffee into Braydon's face."

"She's bound to have heard. Besides—" She bit off her words. Percy should understand she had no desire to accidentally run into Braydon out at the ranch. In all likelihood, he never wanted to see her again after being made a fool of in front of his nearest and dearest.

Whether she admitted it or not, Percy's words struck a nerve. Growing up with nine brothers, she'd not had a lot of female companionship at the winery. And then at Oxford, well, female students were few and far between there. Throwing in her lot with Percy to travel around hunting treasure was not exactly conducive to forging tight female friendships, either.

Bullet had felt different. The time she spent with Laura and Amanda had helped fill a void, provide something that had been missing in her life. By ridiculing Braydon, she had effectively shut the door on any chance of friendship with those ladies.

Here in the west, blood was definitely thicker.

She was on her way to the café, when she heard someone nearby call her name. She looked over to see a familiar rig with Laura and Amanda at the reins. Amanda guided the rig to a stop next to her.

"Where are you off to?" Laura asked.

Maybe they didn't know about the other night. "No place special. Percy is driving me crazy," Henrietta admitted.

"Hop in," Amanda said. "We're off on a little secret excursion."

Beyond intrigued, Henrietta clambered aboard and wedged herself into the makeshift back seat.

"Sorry, it's kind of squishy back there," Amanda said, as she flicked the reins.

"Not a problem," Henrietta said. "Where are we off to?"

Laura turned around with an excited smile. "First you must swear an oath of secrecy."

Intrigued, Henrietta raised her pinkie finger. "Swear."

"We're off to inspect a parcel of land not far from the café."

Henrietta leaned forward, resting her arms along the back of Laura's front seat.

"To what purpose?"

"Have you seen the dance hall in Yuma?" Amanda asked over her shoulder, as she steered the rig around a stagecoach of disembarking passengers near the livery.

Henrietta thought back to her evening in Yuma with Braydon. "I've walked past. Not much truck with dancing these days," she said. "Or ever, for that matter."

"There's more to it than just dancing," Laura said. "Bullet needs something in the area. A place for meetings and gatherings and socializing."

"A place Hawkes doesn't have his finger in," Amanda said, darkly.

"Hawkes's name is like a dirty word around here. Why does he have so much influence?"

"Historically, bad things have happened to anyone who chanced to get in his way."

"I guess that includes me now," Henrietta said. She shivered slightly, remembering those men who had accosted her and Percy on their way to camp. The way the fat one looked at her. She hadn't thought much of it at the time, but she had heard them mention Hawkes's name.

"It's all of us, really," Laura said. "The Masons hate him as much as he hates them. There's been more than one showdown over the years, with Brody doing his best to halt the spread of terror. Our next-door neighbors were just forced to sell, probably to him. Brody was really upset about it."

"All the brothers were," Amanda said. "Here it is, just up ahead." She drew the rig to a halt, let out a sigh, and sat admiring the chunk of land. A few sun-bleached boards lay strewn about, as if someone had once started to build a structure but had given up and walked away.

Personally, Henrietta didn't see much to write home about. The town's sidewalks ended some ways back. The road in front was rutted. Very few vehicles drove past. Stray chunks of paper blew across the sandy surface where weeds and scraggy brush fought for survival.

"Sorry, but I don't really see the attraction."

"It's the only vacant building lot in town that Hawkes doesn't own. The road runs right past," Amanda said. There was no mistaking her enthusiasm.

"And it's been cleared and leveled once," Laura said. "It won't need much work to be ready to build on."

"Who would want to build here?" Henrietta asked. From what she knew of the Masons, they were ranchers through and through. She couldn't see any of them getting involved in starting a town business.

"Come on." Amanda bounded down. Laura clambered a little more slowly. Henrietta jumped down agilely next to them.

"How is it you're in town and not out at your camp?" Laura asked.

"Percy is turning into a regular mother hen. He won't let me go out there alone, not after what happened near the ranch on the night of the wedding and those layabouts we ran into."

"Probably wise," Laura said. "Brody has become even more protective than normal since then. And the well being poisoned."

"Your well was poisoned?" Henrietta's jaw fell. "Is everyone all right?"

Laura nodded. "It was an old well, not the one we use these days. Bradley got the water tested in the newer one, and it's fine. Brody suspects Hawkes is behind it. Part of his goal to one day own Copper Moon."

Henrietta thought about those assayers' marks she'd seen out in the caves. Maybe it was high time she had a little chat with Brody Mason herself.

She followed the other two in their inspection of the land.

"Front door here," Amanda said, drawing a rough squiggle in the dry sandy dirt with the toe of her boot. "What do you think, Laura? One story or two?"

Laura stepped back and squinted at the spot, as if drawing it in her mind. "I think two. The upstairs could always be used for offices and storage. And if you need to expand, the option would be there."

"Who's building this supposed structure?" Henrietta asked.

"We are!" Amanda said, with glee. "Well, not really building it. We'll hire carpenters for that part. Once it's built, I'll be in charge, and be able to run it exactly the way I see fit."

"It all started," Laura said, "when Amanda came up with the idea."

"I saw the dance hall in Yuma and it really got me thinking," Amanda said. "Plus, I saw what happened when Georgina expanded her café, and how successful she has become."

"Kind of like 'build it and they will come'?" Henrietta said.

"Exactly."

"And the secrecy part?"

"We're planning to do it without any help from the men. This will be my project. To succeed or fail through my own efforts."

Laura turned to her. "Henrietta, you're a woman ahead of her time. Educated. Adventurous. Well-traveled. You even dress in a way that makes sense."

Henrietta pondered Laura's words. "There's truth in what you say. There's also truth in the fact that I'm not sure I would have undertaken this life if not for Percy. A woman alone has a lot of strikes against her."

"Exactly!" Amanda said. "But a group of women supporting each other, that's a different matter. It worked with Georgina. We've also been talking to Storm. Trying to figure how we can make what she does with her mobile book-lending library even better."

Laura laughed and patted Henrietta's arm. "Don't look so surprised. Surely you didn't think I'd be content sitting out at the ranch knitting baby clothes for the rest of my life?"

"I never really thought much about it," Henrietta admitted.

"It's a new world, my friend. Full of new possibilities."

When they dropped Henrietta off at the house later that day, Henrietta realized she hadn't given Braydon a single thought all day.

CHAPTER 9

B raydon arrived at the church and dismounted, loosely wrapping the horse's reins on a railing near the front entrance. As he followed the winding pathway along the far side of the building, he slid one hand into his pocket and fingered the curling edges of the note Zara had given him showing him where his mother was buried.

He'd not been to a cemetery before, and was unprepared for the endless sea of headstones that greeted him behind the church. Now he knew why Zara had drawn him the map. He carefully eased it from his pocket so it didn't tear, and smoothed it out. Mary Quinn. All of his life, his mother had been a nameless, faceless mystery, and he was still getting used to her name.

The cemetery was crowded and the map not easy to follow. He took a lot of wrong lefts and rights as he wound his way through the graves, some of which were marked with only a rough, wooden cross and nothing else. No name or date. Dry grass and weeds bordered the stones, many of which were so faded they were hard to read. He swallowed thickly at the sight of several small graves close together, identical headstones all bearing the same last name. What a tragedy for the family.

Eventually he found the one he was looking for, a newer stone among the rest, with her name and dates of birth and death still legible. He knelt and traced the numbers with the tip of one finger. She'd died last year. If he'd pressed Zara sooner ...

He shook his head and removed his hat. No point thinking along those lines. Even if they'd met when she was alive, what would he have to say to her?

Why didn't you want me?

He bowed his head and cleared his throat, but no words came. He'd like to believe there was some sort of afterlife, that she was happy there. He glanced up and around. What was he even doing here? The headstone next to hers bore the name Paul Quinn, with a date of death a few years previous. Her husband?

For sure not Braydon's father. According to Zara, both his parents were dead. He'd never know who had sired him. And he didn't give a rat's ass. Not any more than Mary Quinn had given a rat's ass about him. Cast him aside like yesterday's dirty laundry with instructions to dump him in the orphanage so she could go back to her nice, normal life without the added embarrassment of her mistake.

"I didn't ask to be born," he said aloud.

"No one does," said a soft, female voice from behind him.

He jumped up and faced a young woman carrying a straggly handful of wilted flowers. He felt a sudden stab of guilt. He hadn't given a thought to bringing flowers on his visit. Mary might not have been much of a mother to him, but he wasn't much of a son, either.

"Sorry," the girl said softly. "I didn't mean to disturb you."

"Doesn't matter," he said, shoving his hat back on his head. "I'm done here."

The girl nodded. "It's peaceful here. I come fairly often. It soothes me to think of my parents together again. In a better place."

"Your folks are buried here?"

She pointed. "Paul and Mary Quinn. I'm named Paula, after my father."

Braydon blanched, unable to look away. The girl he faced was kind of gangly and plain, probably in her late teens. And if what she said was true, related to him by blood.

HAWKES SQUINTED at the cards in his hand. Tonight's game was not going in his favor. Just when he needed a big win. Randall and Don Lucas, his investors, were putting the screws to him, hinting that they would soon take matters into their own hands if they didn't see some forward movement.

They had no idea what they were up against. No one did. The Masons had tightened their focus and doubled their guard. These days, nothing was getting past them on the ranch. A bunch of women on the ranch ought to have made them sloppy and careless, but just the opposite had occurred.

"You in or out?" the dealer asked.

Hawkes put on his best bluff-face. "Hit me." Desperate times called for desperate measures.

"You ain't got nothin' to bet," one of the players pointed out.

Hawkes pulled out the deed to his ranch. "Except the most valuable piece of real estate in the entire state."

"Hell, I don't want no land. This is a cash game," said one of the others.

"I'll cover off for Mr. Hawkes," said the smooth-talking, well-dressed stranger at the end of the table."

Hawkes smirked. About time someone had a little faith in old Guy Hawkes. Past time. "You won't be sorry," he told the man.

"No, I don't believe I will."

PERCY FOUND Brody outside the barn at the Copper Moon. "Braydon around anywhere?" he asked, as he dismounted.

"Not right now," Brody told Percy. "Not sure what's been eating him lately, but I told him to take a break. Is there a message?"

Percy pressed his lips together. "I guess you don't know when he'll be back."

Brody turned to his horse and pulled off its saddle which he threw over a nearby fence railing. "For all I know, he's gone into Yuma to blow off some steam and won't be back until tomorrow."

"No worries, then. I'll catch up with him some other time." Percy remounted and made his way back to town, hoping to beat Henny back to the house. He wasn't much of an actor, and she'd never believe his claims of ill health if she spotted him out and about.

It hadn't taken much convincing on Henrietta's part to get Percy back out to their camp. He appeared to be getting as antsy as she was in town. Truth be told, she was happier away from Bullet. The town and its inhabitants served as one more reminder of how she didn't fit in.

Not here.

Not anywhere.

And as much as she admired Amanda and Laura for their determination to be something other than someone's wife, she truly wondered just how practical it was.

Georgina might be managing fine as a spinster running the cafe, but once Laura and Amanda had a child or two monopolizing their time, how could they hope to do that and be involved in any sort of business undertaking as well?

She left Percy at the base camp, where he promised to take it easy, before she headed out to the dig site. This routine lasted for several uneventful days, before Percy insisted he was well enough to accompany her. Side by side, they continued the painstaking work of sifting through the dirt and sand and analyzing every little find that might tell them they were getting close to Juan de Iturbe's buried ship.

"I thought treasure hunting was supposed to be exciting," Henrietta said, after a particularly hot and grueling day, as she stood and stretched her stiff back muscles. Too many days hunched over digging, followed by hot, sleepless nights on her uncomfortable camp cot weren't doing her any favors. "Isn't that the bag of goods you sold me so I would join up with you?"

Percy snorted. "You begged me to bring you along on that first excursion to Greece."

"I brought you good luck," Henrietta said. "At least that's what you told me when we found those gravesites on that deserted island."

"The fisherman who took us over on his boat couldn't believe it," Percy said. "Shipwrecked sailors, right under his nose all those years."

"And a nice cache of jewels and gold coins," Henrietta said. "Enough of a haul to convince your benefactor to send us to Egypt."

"Which was a bust," Percy said gloomily. "We'd better find something here soon."

"We will." She paused. "I told Braydon we usually bring in a crew once we find hard evidence that we're in the right location. He said the Masons might agree to be our work crew to save having a bunch of strangers invading the ranch." She didn't add that it would be a ready excuse to have Braydon around. Was he still mad at her for taking him down a peg?

"Not a bad idea," Percy said. "Think you can persuade them?"

"Me?" Her voice rose unintentionally. "Why do I have to do the persuading?"

"Because you're the one who made a fool of Braydon in front of the others."

Henrietta dismissed his words with a wave of her hand. "Braydon made a fool of himself, all by himself. He didn't need any help from me." She pushed back a damp tendril of hair that insisted on falling in her eyes. "My body is telling me I've done enough for one day. I'm going to the river to clean up. You coming?"

"I'm going to keep at this a little longer," Percy said. "I have a feeling we're getting close."

"Suit yourself." Henrietta saddled up and headed to where part of the river had been diverted to irrigate the ranch land. On the other side of the irrigated fields, Braydon had showed her the location of their swimming hole.

BRAYDON CAME UPON PERCY, crouched low in the dig, so intent on his findings that he didn't hear the horse and rider approach.

"Whatcha got there?"

Percy grabbed his rifle, whirled, then visibly relaxed as he recognized him. "Anyone ever tell you not to sneak up on a bloke?"

"I was calling your name before I even dismounted. You were pretty engrossed." Braydon peered over the other man's shoulder. "Wooden pieces from a ship?"

Percy stood, wiping his hands on his trousers. "That's what I'm hoping. Once I analyze the type of wood, that should tell me where the ship was from. Maybe even how old it is."

Braydon let out a low whistle. "I have to say, I was a tad cynical about this treasure-hunting stuff when you first arrived."

"That's typical of most folks. What brings you out this way?"

Braydon kept his voice casual. "Brody mentioned you were by the ranch the other day. I had some time, so thought I'd stop by and see what's up." In spite of himself his gaze stretched across the space, seeking out Henrietta's familiar, willowy form.

He must have been not very subtle about it. "Hen's not here," Percy said. "She went down to the river to clean up."

Braydon's insides clenched at the thought of Henrietta, stripped down to some unmentionable underpinnings in the swimming hole, all damp and fresh from her efforts. She'd smell sweet. And taste even sweeter.

"Are you sure she's all right on her own?" he couldn't stop himself from asking.

"It's been extremely quiet out here all week," Percy said.

Braydon's eyes continued to scour the landscape. "Quiet at the ranch as well. Kind of makes me get up my guard, waiting and watching for the next attack."

"You're sure it's Hawkes who's on the attack?"

"Him and whatever low-life he's convinced to do his dirty work," Braydon said. "Brody's pretty jumpy these days."

"I guess that stands to reason when a man's got a family to think about, not just himself."

Braydon cocked his head. "What brought you to the ranch the other day?"

Percy licked his lips, opened and closed his mouth a few times. "I, uh ... I'm not sure exactly how to say this, old chum. That night at the ranch house. Henrietta's actions toward you. That could have been some of my fault."

Instantly on guard, Braydon watched as Percy swallowed thickly. "How so?"

Percy cleared his throat. "I might have mentioned overhearing something about a little wager between you and your brothers."

"Are you saying she knew all along what I was up to?" Braydon said.

Percy nodded.

"And she played me."

"To be fair, mate, you were playing her first. Weren't you?"

Braydon fell silent. Had he been? It's true, the situation had started out as a lark, a way to break through Henrietta's crusty façade. But then she'd opened up to him that night in Yuma, given him a glimpse of the woman she truly was.

He'd enjoyed getting to know her as they worked out here together. He'd gone from mild curiosity to being truly intrigued by every new aspect of Henrietta he got to know. Particularly her unplumbed secrets and fears.

She had been like a wild horse, all skittish and suspicious to start with. But once you gain the horse's trust, a man could get the ride of a lifetime. He'd been looking forward to that ride with Henrietta. Until she'd turned on him.

Percy was watching him closely. "I've known Hen a long time now. She's not nearly as independent as she makes out to be. She needs a strong man. One who knows how to rein her in, and when to let her have her head."

"What makes you think I'm that man?"

"I didn't say that. But I'd feel badly if I, somehow, got in the way of the two of you finding out."

"Thanks," Braydon said curtly, before he turned and mounted up. He bobbed his head toward the dig site. "Let me know what you find out about the wood."

"I will. Hen said maybe the Masons would be for hire if we need you."

"Could be."

"Where are you headed now?" Percy asked.

"I think it's time Henny and I had us a little chat. One without any witnesses this time."

Henrietta was luxuriating in the handful of suds she had coaxed from the sliver of soap from her saddle bag as she rubbed her fingers through her damp hair, separating the strands from tangling, before she ducked underneath to rinse them.

She felt like a new woman. Almost. As if she'd managed

to wash Braydon out of her hair along with the grime and dust of the dig site. The blouse that she'd washed was drying over some bushes near the shore. The sun's warmth kissed her bare shoulders and the top of her head as she slowly waded out of the water in her underpinnings.

She pulled the small drying flannel from her saddlebag and started to towel off, when she heard the sound of horse and rider coming her way fast. Percy would never ride that fast in this heat.

She reached for her rifle, and held it at the ready, even after the horse and rider were close enough to identify. "What are *you* doing here?" she snarled at Braydon.

"Henny, put the damn gun down so we can talk."

"I don't want to talk. I most certainly don't want to talk when I'm half-dressed and soaking wet."

Braydon ignored her and dismounted. She raised the gun warningly.

Her actions did nothing to halt his long-legged stride in her direction.

"Stay back," she said. "I mean it."

"I'm sure you do." He reached her side and wrested the gun from her. "Never point a gun at a man if you don't intend to fire."

"It's not loaded," she said gracelessly, noticing that he checked anyway. Clearly, he didn't believe her.

"Even more foolhardy," Braydon said. "What if I'd been someone out to do you harm?"

"I have my pistol right here. I'm a better up-close shot with that."

She grew self-conscious as Braydon stood looking at her, slowly shaking his head, a bemused expression tugging at his handsome features, as if he couldn't quite believe she was here. Or he was. That they both were.

"What am I going to do with you?"

"Do with me? Nothing. I believe I made that quite clear the other evening."

"The only thing you made clear is what an intriguing, exasperating little thing you are. Managed to beat me at my own game. Or so you thought."

"What do you mean?'

"I mean somewhere along the line, it stopped being a game. It started to feel very, very real."

"I don't know what you're talking about."

He tangled his hands through her loose, wet hair, urging her gaze up to his. "I think you do. I think you know exactly what I'm talking about. This."

His kiss was hard and punishing, as if he didn't really want to kiss her but couldn't stop himself. Beneath the embrace, she sensed a man in conflict. Wanting her, even as he hated himself for wanting her.

Heady stuff indeed.

Because she wanted him with the same urgent fervency. The pleasure of the forbidden. The desperate wanting of something you know is bad for you. Which only made the taking all the more sweet.

"Damn you," he said against her lips, without breaking contact.

"Damn you, too," she said, pulling back ever so slightly to catch her breath. "Wooing me in order to win your dumb bet."

"What bet?" he said. "All I want is this. The ultimate prize. You in my arms. Trembling with need. Breathless with desire."

Her breath caught; her heart raced as his hands moved from her shoulders and down her bare arms. The heat of his touch warmed her cool, damp skin before she felt his hands span her waist.

She was near-naked in her wet underthings, her nipples clearly visible through the damp lawn of her chemise, a fact Braydon was quick to notice.

He pressed his face to the top of her head and took a long sniff. "You smell amazing. Is that honeysuckle?"

"Jasmine," she said.

"Exotic as you are."

Henrietta smiled against the front of his shirt. No one had ever called her exotic before.

"We'd better get back," Braydon said, with a regretful sigh. "Percy found something he wants to show you."

Dusk had begun to fall by the time they reached the dig site, where Percy waited impatiently for their return. "You have to see this, Hen."

She knelt down, picked up a soft brush and started to brush away another layer of sand from what appeared to be several lengths of wood from the mast of a ship.

Heart pounding, she looked up at Percy. "We found it!" she said reverently. She wanted to claw away, dig down fast and hard, but she held off. That wasn't the way these things were done.

"We don't know for sure it's from Juan's ship," Percy said. "I need to take this back to town for further analysis."

Excitement raced through her veins. Braydon stood nearby, one hand extended to help her to her feet. Life was getting complicated and interesting all at once. She smiled up at him. "Do you think your brothers would be willing to come out and help us? If this, in fact, does prove genuine?"

"I'd wager you'd have a hard time keeping us away."

BRAYDON COULDN'T QUITE fathom what was happening or how he felt about it, as he escorted Henrietta and Percy back to the house where they stayed in town. As soon as they arrived, Percy scampered away with his precious artifact, leaving Braydon and Henrietta alone in the barn.

He noticed her hands weren't quite steady as she removed her mount's bridle. She appeared to focus all of her attention on the task at hand, while he preferred her attention be focused on him. She bent down to loosen the cinch on the saddle. When she straightened and reached for the saddle, he beat her to it, lifting the saddle off with one easy movement.

"I can do this myself, you know."

Amused, he smiled down at her, noticing the excited flush to her cheeks and the way her eyes shone in the dim lantern light. "I know. You can manage everything on your own. But what if you don't always need to?"

Henrietta leaned on the post at one corner of the horse's stall. "Nothing good can come of this, Braydon."

"This, what?"

"This." She spread her hands flat as if smoothing an imaginary surface. "You being intrigued by me because I'm different from most other women. Me getting used to having you do things for me."

"I like doing things for you."

"And one day I'll no longer be here. Wherever I am, I'll have to get used to doing for me all over again."

One day she wouldn't be here.

He didn't like the sound of that.

"Does it have to work that way? Once you find what you came here for, you move on without a backward glance?"

She picked up a brush and started grooming her horse. "It's the only way I know."

"And you never think about settling down? Staying in one place to put down some roots?"

"I had roots," she said. "It was like a chokehold."

He cocked his head and studied her, wondering about her secrets. What happened in her past that made her this way.

"Do you ever think about going home?"

"Back to Argentina?" She gave her head a swift, emphatic shake. But not fast enough that he failed to see the bright sheen of unshed tears. Something he said had dredged up sad memories.

He moved to her side and took the brush from her unresisting fingers.

"Bad memories back in Argentina?"

She raised her chin in that fashion he so admired. Determined. Challenging. "Not all bad."

He shrugged. "You know where you came from. And who came before you. For me, I found out too late."

Her mouth opened in a wide "O", her eyes full of questions. "Your mother?"

"Buried out in Yuma." He paused. "Appears I have a half-sister."

She squeezed his arm. "That's wonderful, Braydon. You have to find her. She can tell you things."

"I can't do that," he said shortly.

"Why not?"

"Because her knowing me would change everything she knows about her mother. Right now, she has that short lifetime of memories. Something I have no right to take from her."

"You don't think she'd be excited to learn she has a brother she never knew about? Especially with her mother gone?"

"Would you?"

"I have too many brothers as it is."

"How would you feel if you learned your mother lived her entire life, yet kept a huge secret from you?"

"I'd expect she had her reasons."

"Well, that's not how most folks would think. Most folks would feel betrayed and lied to. And nothing they can do about it with the parent cold in the ground, except resent them for living a lie."

She cocked her head, as if seeing him for the first time. "This is something I would not have expected from you, Braydon. To think of others before yourself."

"Which is something I didn't learn until after I hooked up with Brody and the rest of them. Before that, I was a selfish bastard. I didn't care who I hurt." He cupped her chin in his hand. "That's how you can be sure I'd never hurt you, Henny." He ran a gentle finger across her lips. "I'm sorry about that stupid bet. It didn't mean anything."

Braydon left Henrietta in more of a quandary than she would have dreamt possible. It was as if the Braydon she had first met had changed right before her eyes. Morphed into someone completely different. Someone she longed to know better.

She pushed the thought away. There was no room in her life for getting to know folks better. For starting to care. There was no room in her life for anything except moving on to the next grand adventure.

Before long she'd be gone from this place. Laura would have her baby. Amanda would maybe start up her music hall. Eventually, the other Mason boys would get married and start families. Everyone she'd met here would grow and flourish.

While she grew old alone.

CHAPTER 10

News tended to travel fast in Bullet. Especially when it concerned a dead body. Even when that body was found as far away as Yuma.

When Braydon heard rumors that the dead girl was maybe somehow linked to Madam Zara's establishment, he was saddled up and on his way to Yuma in record time. Zara and her girls were no stranger to the sheriff and deputy blundering around the premises, both for business and pleasure, but he felt he needed to check in and make sure nothing went sideways.

It was late when he arrived. Inside, the place was about as lively as a morgue. No music. No customers. Just a parlor full of really sad ladies, sharing hankies to wipe away their tears.

"Zara. I came as soon as I heard." He squatted next to her and took her hand in both of his. It felt cold as ice.

Zara dabbed at her eyes with her free hand, which only smeared the kohl liner and made her look like a racoon. Braydon passed her his handkerchief, and she blew her nose loudly.

"That's mighty kind of you, Braydon. Ain't nothing you can do. Ain't nothing any of us can do for that poor girl now. And why anyone would want to hurt her ... " She gave way to a fresh outpouring of sobs.

"Any of her customers get mad or get rough?" Braydon asked.

"Braydon, you know for a fact none of us entertains that sort of man here. No one has ever been hurt here, let alone killed, in all the years my doors have been open."

Braydon knew from his youth that Zara spoke the truth.

"Besides." Zara paused to gulp in a shaky breath. "Paula wasn't working here. Not like that. She just played the piano for us sometimes." She waved a shaky hand at the silent instrument. "Can't hardly bear to look at it without remembering her sitting there, sweet as a pea. Innocent as an angel." She hiccupped. "She'd been staying here a spell since her ma passed. Getting over her grief and all."

All of a sudden she looked at him, let out a little gasp and clapped both hands to her mouth.

Slowly Braydon rose to his full height. "What did you say her name was?"

Zara pressed her lips together in a thin line and looked up at him with sorrowful eyes.

"Paula Quinn. Is that right? Daughter of Mary Quinn?"

Zara looked down at the soggy hankie on her lap and twisted it into knots. For the first time, he noticed how old her hands looked, the knuckles so swollen she could no longer wear all the rings she used to deck herself out in.

"That's right," she whispered.

"I saw her once," he said. "She was just a girl. Who would want to hurt her?" He skewered Zara with his gaze. "You have any trouble here with anyone lately?"

She worried her lower lip. "Hawkes was here not long

ago. Drunk as a skunk. Asking for Dolly. He didn't take too kindly when I threw him out. Well, Robert did. My days of strong-arming the customers are behind me."

"So Robert threw him out. Do you remember if Paula was here that night? Did he see her?"

"'Spect he did. She played most every night. I think it helped her with her grieving."

"You tell this to the sheriff?"

She gave her head a jerky shake. "You know Hawkes is tight with the sheriff here."

"Here and everywhere else in these parts," Braydon said.

Zara lowered her voice so none of the others could hear. "Did you get a chance to talk to Paula? You said you saw her once."

"I saw her at the cemetery. Exchanged a few words is all. I didn't figure it was the time or the place to mention the fact that we had the same mother. Let her keep her memories of her mother the way she knew her."

Zara looked relieved. "It would for sure have been confusing for her."

"Any of the ladies here know of my connection to Paula?"

"Not really. Not many of us left from the old days. Why?"

"Any chance one of them might have said something to Hawkes?"

"What are you getting at, Braydon?'

"I'm thinking, if Hawkes had her killed, it might have been nothing to do with you or her. And everything to do with me."

At Zara's insistence, Braydon agreed to spend the night in his old room. But before he turned in, he made the rounds of the local saloons and gambling halls, keeping his ears open. Seemed like the entire town was abuzz with talk of the murder. He learned Paula's body been found in a wooded area between town and the church.

Everywhere he went, he heard folks speaking, low-voiced, about "the poor thing"- "Not an enemy in the world"- "Kept to herself"- "Lost after her ma passed"-

It didn't sound as if anyone knew Paula had been spending her time at Zara's. Of course, he thought cynically. If any of the town husbands had seen her there, they weren't about to be blabbing that to the women folk.

His old bed was awful short, and his feet hung over the edge. His old room was mostly used for storage. Next day he was up and in the saddle early, long before anyone in the house was stirring.

Bullet was mostly asleep when he reached the town. Instead of heading for the ranch, he found himself outside Amanda's house where Percy and Henny were staying.

He sat on his horse, quietly watching the sun's early rays hit the side of the building. There was no sign of life. For all he knew, Percy and Henrietta had gone back out to the camp. Unanswered questions whirled through his brain. Who had killed Paula? And why? And even more unsettling, why was Henny the only one he felt he could talk to about it?

"Are you planning to sit there on your horse all day staring at the house, or come up to the porch like a gentleman?"

Recognizing Henrietta's voice, he blinked in the sunlight and squinted in the direction of the porch. Vaguely, he made out her form in the shadows at the far end, where she blended into the wicker chair as if she wasn't even there.

"I didn't want to disturb anyone in case you were still asleep." He dismounted and climbed the stairs slowly, hat in hand.

She took one critical look at him. "You look like you could use some coffee. Take a seat."

She was back in less than a minute with a steaming cup in one hand. He blew on the hot contents, then took a grateful sip. The brew was milky and sweet, just the way he liked it. He wondered how she knew that. There were a lot of things he wondered how she knew.

"Didn't get much sleep," he said, in response to her unasked question.

She didn't press him for further information, just let him sip his coffee and reflect, as if she knew he'd speak up when he had a mind to.

"I thought you might be out at the camp."

"Percy's still fussing around like an old woman with that chunk of wooden mast we brought back. He's figured out what kind of wood it is, but not what time period the boat was likely in service. Things like that make him crazy when he can't find the answers he's looking for."

"I kind of get that," Braydon said.

"Funny," Henrietta said. "You and Percy are more alike than one would expect upon first meeting the two of you."

"Hardly," Braydon said with a snort. "He's a scholar. I'm just a rancher cowpoke with a limited education."

"Life skills and people skills hold a body in lot better stead than all the book learning in the world."

"I'm surprised to hear you say that."

She gifted him with that radiant, self-amused smile he loved. "Of course, I had to go to Oxford to figure it out."

"You miss it? The higher learning?"

"Not a bit. These days I'm focused on learning what I can about people. Which is proving a lot more complicated."

"I'm just a simple guy."

She shook her head slowly, her gaze warm on his. "Secrets, Braydon. Secrets upon secrets. Showing folks only what you want them to see. Take right now. You're clearly not of a mind to share what kept you awake all night. Or has you here so early this morning."

"A young woman was killed in Yuma the other day. I'm worried it might somehow have something to do with me."

She curled her feet up underneath her bent legs in the wicker chair as if she was settling in to listen.

HAWKES GAVE a satisfied belch as he finished his breakfast. Nothing like a fresh kill to help a man sleep like a baby. Maybe he'd made a mistake in recent years, sending others to do whatever killing needed to be done.

He'd taken it as a sure-fire sign when he'd seen that little gal from Zara's trotting along the road outside of town by her lonesome. How he had enjoyed watch her friendly smile fade to terror, and then emptiness, as he put his hands around her fragile windpipe and squeezed the life from her.

He hadn't felt this good since the night years ago, when he'd killed that idiot who worked for him. The one who had the twin brothers, now friendly with those Mason scum. Fondly he stroked the homemade knife he'd taken off his victim as a keepsake. He'd felt plumb naked in jail without it. And he'd make damn good and sure he never ended up there again.

He reached in his pocket and pulled out his latest keepsake. He hadn't taken it from his victim, but had planted its mate on her body. The light hit the ruby stone in the earring turning it to the satisfying color of blood.

He wouldn't be keeping this matching bauble. No, sir. He

intended to plant it where it would do the most good. Screw with the Mason bastards the way they'd screwed with him.

WHEN HENRIETTA HAD FIRST NOTICED Braydon in the street out front, she'd had to look twice in case she had conjured him up out of thin air. She'd been up early, unable to sleep, thanks to Braydon invading her dreams. Last night she dreamt they were a couple, sharing a life of laughter and love. It was a nice dream. One in which she'd felt safe. Loved and secure. Nothing about the dream matched the life she had created for herself.

She'd been sad to hear of the young girl's death.

Braydon would never understand if he learned she'd met Paula

Quinn a few days ago. She'd run into the young woman out at the cemetery near Yuma.

How could she possibly explain what she had been doing there when she wasn't even sure herself?

She'd traveled there after Braydon told her about his mother, as if a grave and headstone might hold some clues regarding the man before her. She needed to know what it was about Braydon that drew her in. Made her want to learn more about him.

Learn everything about him.

She couldn't even explain her actions to herself.

Paula had been at the cemetery when she arrived, and they'd had a nice chat. The poor thing had seemed very much alone, and Henrietta left scheming how she might get Braydon to meet with his sister and disclose their relationship. Personally, she felt it would bring the young woman comfort to know she wasn't totally alone in the world.

It also wouldn't hurt Braydon to take on the role of big brother.

"Why would you think her death might have something to do with you?"

"It all goes back to Hawkes. The way he preys on folks who are weaker as a way to get to us."

"You think he found out there was a connection between the girl who was killed and you?"

Braydon gave her a sharp glance. "I didn't say there was a connection between me and the dead girl."

Henrietta bit down hard on her lower lip. She needed to watch what she said around Braydon. He was nobody's fool. "It only stands to reason. The other day you told me you have a sister. Now you say this girl's death might have something to do with you. It's clear you feel guilty and broken up because you weren't there for her. Didn't protect her. You're not likely to feel that way about some random stranger."

He reached out and caught her hand in his. It was a sweet gesture. Drawing close to her, but in a caring, nonthreatening way, as if he needed the touch of another human. "I forget how smart you are. So much more on your mind than fashion and parties and babies and the like."

She linked her fingers through his. Something felt so right about her hand mated with his. "Smart enough to outfox you at your own game."

He pretended to give her a hang-dog look. "That stupid bet. Are you ever going to let me forget about that?"

She tossed her head and gave him her smug, superior smile. "Seems unlikely. You were a very poor loser."

He scooted his chair closer so his knees brushed hers. "I was not. I paid up right away."

"And the brothers all thanked me. All except Brody. I

think he was miffed to be left out of the joke in the first place."

"He would have told Laura. There are no secrets between those two. And her being a woman, she would more than likely have tipped you off, if Percy hadn't already spilled."

She fell silent. No secrets between Brody and Laura. Is that how married life worked? She glanced from their linked hands to Braydon's sincere gaze on hers. "Are secrets such a bad thing?"

He exhaled loudly, no doubt lost in thoughts of his mother, his sister. And everything that had been kept from him his entire life. "I think they can be dangerous. Sometimes even deadly."

"You had nothing to do with that poor young woman's death, Braydon. For that matter, it could have been a random passer-by who killed her. Nothing to do with Hawkes at all."

"When you've lived in Bullet as long as I have, you learn everything bad is somehow linked back to Hawkes."

"Morning, folks. Hope I'm not intruding."

Henrietta snatched her hand from Braydon's. She didn't know the tall, gray-haired stranger, but he was making his way up the steps as if he had every right to be there.

Braydon stood, fists clenched, limbs coiled as if he was ready to spring to her defense. "And who might you be?"

Just then, Henrietta saw sunlight bounce off the badge the man wore pinned to his chest.

"I'm Marshal Philips."

"I haven't seen you around these parts before," Braydon said. There was a challenge in his tone.

"Normally they keep me plenty busy out in Tucson. I'm

here right now investigating the murder of a young lady over in Yuma. You might have heard?"

"Bad news always travels fast," Braydon said. "Which in no way explains what brings you to Bullet."

"I've been ordered to take over the investigation." The man stroked the silver moustache on his upper lip. "Fair bit of politics involved. The girl had been reported missing. Appears she's got relatives in high places."

Braydon raised a brow. "I don't see Sheriff Yates cottoning much to playing second fiddle."

"Yates is a fool. His superior in Yuma is not much better. But as long as the locals keep voting those buffoons into office, everyone's stuck with them, including my bosses."

Henrietta watched the interaction between the men, like two dogs circling each other warily, each unsure if the other was friend or foe.

"There have been a lot of unsolved murders happen out this way in the past that no one seemed to care about," Braydon said.

"That's why I'm involved. This time people care."

"People who matter," Braydon said bitterly.

Henrietta wondered if he made the connection that the victim's relatives in high places could also be his relatives in high places.

"It's an imperfect system," Philips said. "Folks in government are trying to change that."

"How can we help?" Henrietta asked, in an effort to defuse what was looking to be a tense situation.

"I was hoping you might help identify something that was found at the crime scene." Philips reached in his vest pocket and pulled out a familiar-looking ruby earring.

Henrietta's eyes flew to Braydon, then back to the earring. "Why did you bring this to me?"

KATHLEEN LAWLESS

"Got an anonymous tip led us to Bullet. Lady over at the café suggested this might belong to you," Philips said. "It's a pretty valuable piece for most folks' budgets in these parts."

"May I?" At his nod, Henrietta plucked the earring from the lawman's palm and examined it closely, aware Braydon watched her, his face etched with shocked disbelief. Surely, he didn't think she had something to do with the young woman's death.

"It looks like a set that belonged to my grandmother. I don't often wear them."

Braydon's voice was cold. "You were wearing the pair of them out at the ranch the other night."

"Do you by chance know where the other one is?" Philips asked.

She shook her head. "I put them on my dresser when I got home on the night Braydon mentioned. I had planned to lay them away the next day. By the time I remembered, they weren't where I'd left them. I assumed I had simply mislaid them and they'd show up."

Philips nodded, as if what she said confirmed what he already knew. "I guess the next step is to figure out how one ended up in the hands of a dead girl. And where the other one got to."

"You didn't mention your earrings were missing," Braydon said, once the marshal had left.

"I didn't think much of it. Then we were busy at the dig. I expected they'd show up someplace stupid where I had absently misplaced them."

"Did you see any signs of forced entry when you returned from the camp?" Braydon asked.

"Nothing obvious."

"Anything else missing?" he said.

"Not that I noticed. What are you getting at, Braydon?"

"You have to admit, it does look suspicious. You don't notice or say anything when some valuable jewelry, jewelry that belonged to your grandmother no less, goes missing."

Henrietta stood. "I don't care for your insinuation."

"I was only saying—"

"You were implying I might have had something to do with that young woman's death. That she ripped off one of my earrings in our struggle and I've hidden the other one someplace. Can you, even for one second, dream up a motive for me to have done that?"

Braydon visibly slumped. "Of course not, Henny." He straightened, his eyes boring into hers. "But then, all I know about you is what you've chosen to tell me and the rest of the town. No one really knows who you are or where you come from."

She planted her hands on her hips. "That puts me on a par with everyone else who's recently moved to your stupid town. I think you should go now."

"You haven't moved here, Hen. Remember? You're just passing through. You'll take your buried treasure once you find it and move on. You don't care about the people here, or their lives. You're just all caught up in your own selfish game."

Henrietta closed her eyes in an effort to ward off the memories. The raised voices from her past calling her names, accusing her of being selfish. Selfish because she wouldn't bow to their neighbor's attempts to force himself on her. Selfish because she refused to marry the abusive, lying landowner and merge their vineyards. Selfish because she continued to deny his version of events— how she seduced him.

"You're right, Braydon. Henrietta, the selfish one. Henrietta, the murderer of helpless young females. Henrietta, who doesn't care a toss about anyone other than herself."

His face grew pinched with displeasure. She saw a white line form at the edge of his nostrils.

"I'd watch myself if I were you. Your dig site is on Copper Moon land. It wouldn't take much for the lot of us to shut you down. We sure as heck won't be coming to help you. Or sanction you bringing in any work crews, either. You and Percy are all on your own out there."

With that, he turned on his heel and stomped down the front steps.

"What in tarnation was all that yelling about?" Percy asked a few minutes later as he poked his head out the front door. "A ruckus loud enough to wake the dead."

"That, my friend, is what happens when one starts to care about people. To get involved in their lives."

Percy placed one hand heavily on each of her shoulders. "Nothing good ever comes from getting involved, Hen. Why do you think I stay firmly entrenched in the past?"

"Good advice. How's it coming with that chunk of ship's mast? Are we any closer to discovering the vintage of the vessel?"

"Patience, my dear. Rome wasn't built in a day."

No, Henrietta thought. But her heart had been shattered in just under a minute.

CHAPTER 11

Back at the ranch, Braydon threw himself into work with such zeal that everyone, even Brody, started giving him funny looks. Keeping busy was the only way he could stop berating himself for acting such a fool the other day with Henrietta. He knew there was no way she could be connected to Paula Quinn's death.

Out in the back paddocks, checking the fence line gave him plenty of time to reflect. If someone broke in to Henrietta's house and stole her earrings, it had to have been Hawkes. It would be easy enough for the man to plant one at the murder scene in an effort to deflect suspicion from himself and onto Henrietta.

The more he thought about Hawkes trying to implicate Henrietta in the murder, the more incensed he grew. He'd heard through the grapevine that Henrietta and Percy were back out at their camp. A torrent of emotions ran through him. Regret that he wasn't there to help. Excitement for Henrietta that they may have found their treasure. Bleakness at the thought of her soon packing and leaving town.

As usual, he showed up late for the evening meal,

preferring to work till well after sundown. Amanda and Bradley were still at the ranch house with several of the others. Blake sat at the table whittling. Brody and Laura were nowhere to be seen.

"I don't know what you and Henrietta had a fight about," Amanda said when he joined them. "But why don't you do us all a favor and go make amends?"

"Nothing to do with her," Braydon growled as he dished himself up a serving of beans from the pot on the back of the stove. There was a funny-looking misshapen loaf of bread on the sideboard. "What happened here?"

"I was having an off day," Amanda said.

"It was an admirable try, my love," Bradley said quickly.

Braydon almost broke the knife trying to saw through the loaf. The slice felt hard as a brick, but he buttered a slab anyway and took a seat at the table, looking away from the happy couple, who had eyes only for each other. Cynically, he wondered how long love like that lasted.

"How's the new herd settling in?" Bradley asked when he finally managed to rip himself away from the lovestruck exchange of glances with his wife.

Braydon figured the question to be more small talk than actual interest.

"Haven't seen any problems so far. You might head out though one of these days and take a look for yourself. A couple of the females acting like they might be calving round about the same time as Laura."

"Don't dare talk about Laura's condition like that," Amanda snapped. "Have a little respect."

Braydon grinned into his supper dish, having effectively steered the conversation away from himself and Henrietta.

"Heard they sent someone new our way, a marshal from

Tucson, to investigate the death of that poor little gal over in Yuma," Blake said.

Braydon nodded, not bothering to mention how he had met the lawman the other day, or the fact that Henrietta's earring had wound up in the dead girl's hand.

Amanda gave Bradley a wide-eyed look. "Don't tell me. Someone finally figured that crooked sheriff can't be trusted to do a thorough investigation? Someone's getting smart at long last."

"Government's always been like that," Benjamin said, from across the room. "Whatever they do all depends who's in favor at the time."

"Bullet always was a killing town, even before it was much of a town," Amanda said.

"Ever hear how the town got its name?" Benjamin said. "Back in the day, this is where outlaws came to do their killing and dispose of the bodies. Used to tell each other, taking' em over to Bullet to do the deed". Lots of stories from back when the town was first getting settled, that the ground was riddled with bullets."

Amanda grew noticeably pale. Braydon wondered if she was thinking about the father she had never known. The man had disappeared under suspicious circumstances before Amanda was born, his remains never found.

"Well, I hope they find out who killed that girl and bring them to justice," Amanda said.

They were interrupted by a loud knocking on the front door.

Amanda started to rise. "Isn't it kind of late for someone to come calling?"

Bradley's hand on her shoulder stilled her movement. "I'll get it." He stood, one hand on his revolver in its holster.

Braydon swung toward the door, his hand also on his gun, meal forgotten.

"Who's there?" Bradley called.

"Marshal Philips. From over Yuma way."

"Speak of the devil," Blake said.

Braydon and Bradley exchanged glances. Bradley cautiously opened the door and peered out onto the porch. "How can we help you, Marshal?"

"Sorry to be stopping in so late. Looking to have a word with Braydon Mason."

With seeming reluctance, Bradley stepped away from the door as Braydon stood and took his place.

It was dark, but not too dark he couldn't see two other riders hanging back in the shadows. "What's this about?"

"Just following up on what we spoke to the other day. Miss Henrietta's missing earrings. Mind if I come in?"

Hearing Henrietta's name sent a funny ripple through him. He'd been thinking about her all day, but to hear the marshal say her name aloud seemed all wrong.

"Don't know what I can add to what was said the other day," Braydon said stiffly.

"I was hoping you wouldn't mind doing me a favor," the marshal said. "Empty out the contents of your saddlebag."

Braydon took a deep swallow. Something about the way this was going sent a warning chasing down the back of his neck as he picked up a lit lantern. "It's in the barn with my saddle. What's this about?"

"Just doing my due diligence."

"What about them?" Braydon pointed to the other two riders, one of whom he recognized in the dim lamplight as Sheriff Yates, Hawkes's buddy. The second man must be the deputy. "You expecting to need back-up?"

"That wasn't the intent. I wasn't sure I could find the

ranch in the dark. Just wait here for me, fellas," he said when Yates made like he was planning to dismount.

"Appreciate your cooperation," Philips said as he followed Braydon across the yard to the barn.

"I've got nothing to hide." Once inside, Braydon pointed to his saddlebag, still buckled to his saddle. "That one's mine. Fill your boots."

Carefully the marshal removed the bag's contents, which consisted of a bandanna, an extra canteen of water, Braydon's knife and honing stone, a tinder box, a ball of piggin string and an earring.

What the hell!

Braydon had to look twice and still didn't believe his eyes, even as lamplight winked on the ruby's facets, balanced in the palm of the marshal's hand.

"You see this before today?"

"Yes, sir. On Miss Henrietta's ear about a week or so back when she was here at the ranch for supper. Looks identical to the one you had the other day when you stopped by her place."

Marshal Philips sighed heavily. "Stands to reason this is the mate to that other one. I'll need to take it for Miss Henrietta to identify."

"Where's the one you showed us the other day at her place?"

"It's in evidence, back at the sheriff's office."

"You sure about that?"

The marshal gave him a long, level look. "All I'm sure about is that something is definitely not adding up here. I don't like it when my investigations are based on nothing more than a lot of anonymous tips. Kind of makes me feel like I'm being manipulated into a certain way of thinking."

"Lots of things aren't adding up," Braydon said. "Starting

with who put that earring in my saddlebag. And how you knew it would be there."

"Things get weirder than that," the marshal said. "We got us an eye witness who saw Miss Henrietta talking to Paula Quinn. Few days before Miss Quinn turned up dead."

Braydon felt like he'd been sucker-punched. Henny had been seen talking to Paula? Could that be true?

Another disquieting thought ran through his head. Would Henrietta have had the chance to plant the earring in his saddlebag?

The marshal shot him a long, level look. "Funny how I've got not one, but two suspects who, turns out, are friendly with each other."

"Aren't you forgetting something, Marshal? You're sorely lacking any sort of motive."

Marshall nodded. "Evidence is circumstantial at best. Still gotta ask you. Where were you the day Miss Quinn was killed?"

"I was here at the ranch. Ask any of my brothers or their wives."

"I'll be sure and do that. I'll also be looking to find out where Miss Henrietta was at the time of the murder. For now, I suggest you stick around close by. Don't be leaving town or anything. And maybe find yourself a good lawyer, just in case."

Braydon got no sleep that night and was up early the next morning, on his way to Yuma. As before, he went around back of Zara's and in the kitchen door. As usual, Zara sat at the table, her hair in pin curls, last night's makeup smeared across her face.

She looked up. "Braydon. You're getting to be a frequent visitor these days."

"You meet Marshal Philips yet?"

"He's been by several times. Real thorough chap. Not like that idiot of a sheriff. Genuinely cares what happened to Paula."

"Yeah," Braydon agreed absently. "This might seem like a weird question, but did you ever see Miss Henrietta, that treasure-hunter gal from Bullet, around talking to Paula?"

"I never saw any strange woman around the house here, and that's a certainty. Robert makes sure of that."

"Paula ever mention her?"

"Not as I recall."

"Because the marshal seems to think Paula was seen talking to Henrietta shortly before she was killed."

Zara shrugged one plump, rounded shoulder. "It's possible. It's not like I was keeping tabs on the gal or anything. She looked young, but she was old enough to look after herself." Her eyes took on a far-away look Braydon remembered well from his youth. "Now that you mention it, she did say something about running into a nice lady out at the cemetery one day. She was all kind of giddy 'cause this lady wasn't from around here. Had traveled to some crazy foreign lands. I was worried she might be filling Paula's head with romantic nonsense. Ever since her ma died, Paula was a little lost and I didn't want some stranger luring her away, filling her head with glory-days dreams."

Braydon pressed his lips together thoughtfully. So it must be true. Henrietta had been acquainted with Paula. Which sounded far too suspicious to be any sort of a coincidence.

"That sound like your treasure-hunter gal?"

Braydon nodded. "Except she's not my treasure-hunter gal." More and more, he was getting the message Henrietta was either a snoop or a liar. Maybe both.

HAD SHE OVERREACTED TOWARD BRAYDON? For the first time in her life, Henrietta wished she could talk the situation over with some like-minded female friends. But Amanda and Laura both lived at the Copper Moon, and she was hardly about to show up at the ranch. Braydon was just egotistical enough to think she might be hoping to run into him.

As for Percy, her best friend, she could hardly talk to him about matters of the heart. She knew he still felt bad about tipping her off regarding the wager between Braydon and his brothers. As if her knowing what Braydon was up to made any difference to him being a shortsighted jerk who jumped to conclusions. That he might think, even for a second, she had anything to do with that poor girl's death.

She shook her head so vigorously she almost walked straight into a young woman coming toward her. She pulled back just at the last minute.

The woman had her nose stuck in a book.

Henrietta bit back a smile. "Do you always read when you're walking down the street?"

The stranger glanced up, with a tentative smile. "Not normally." She took in Henrietta's apparel. "You must be Henrietta." Her words were tinged with a faint Irish lilt.

At Henrietta's nod, her smile widened. "I'm Storm."

"Of the mobile lending-library fame," Henrietta said.

Storm nodded. "Laura and Amanda speak of you often."

Henrietta wasn't sure what to make of that information. It seemed everyone in town spoke freely about everyone else.

"Don't worry," Storm said. "They only say the nicest things."

Henrietta nodded ruefully. "That sounds like them."

Storm's eyes brightened. "Would you like to see the book wagon?"

Henrietta surprised herself with her answer. "Thank you. I believe I would."

They arrived at the wagon and Henrietta followed Storm into the back of the conveyance, which was a in bit of a higgledy-piggledy disorder.

"I need new shelves and a few things modified so I can organize the books better," Storm said in apology.

Despite the clutter, Henrietta spent a pleasant half hour with Storm, perusing the books and hearing about the many western towns the other woman had visited. At the end of her visit, it seemed only polite to pick out some reading material to take with her.

"Nothing too heavy," she told Storm. "I need light, escape reading." When was the last time she'd sat down to read something that didn't pertain to research and history?

"I think you'll really love this," Storm said. She placed *Anne* by Constance Fenimore Woolson in Henrietta's hand. "It's about the life of a young orphan."

Considering most of the folks she'd met in Bullet were orphans, it seemed a fitting choice.

She arrived home to find Marshal Philips pacing in front of the house. "Oh, good," he said, when she arrived. "Your man said you likely wouldn't be gone long."

"Percy is not 'my man'," she said shortly.

"A mere figure of speech," Philips said. "I happened across something you'll be interested to see."

"You'd best come in then." Henrietta led the way inside, gratified to see Percy had at least made a token effort at tidying things. She put down her borrowed book and turned his way. "What's this about?"

"This." He unwrapped a silk handkerchief and pulled out a familiar-looking ruby earring. "I believe it to be the mate of the one from the crime scene." He passed it her way. "Take your time, miss. Examine it up close. Make good and sure this is one of your missing earrings."

Henrietta barely gave the earring a glance. "I don't need time to examine it closely. I'd know it anywhere. Where did you get it?"

"Turned up in Mr. Braydon Mason's saddlebag." She wasn't fooled by the casual way he watched her reaction. "The two of you looked kind of friendly when I dropped by the other morning. I wanted to be sure you didn't leave the earrings at his place, maybe give them to him to keep for you. Something of that nature. Could be as they pinched your ears so you took them off and left them behind, only thought you wore them back home."

"Mr. Mason's saddlebag! That makes no more sense than one being in the hand of that murdered girl. And no, I did not take them off that night at the Copper Moon. I distinctly recall laying them on top of my dresser on a doily."

Philips nodded. "Darn confusing, I agree."

"If he found it in his bag, why didn't he give it to me? Why give it to you?"

Philips exhaled a weighty sigh. "Nothing so simple, I'm afraid. Mason claims he had no idea it was there."

Henrietta narrowed her gaze. "So what made you go out to search his bag?"

Marshal shuffled and stared down at the tips of his boots. Henrietta absently noticed he'd taken the time to get them shined. "Got an anonymous tip that's where we would find it."

Henrietta narrowed her gaze. "You don't strike me as the type of man to put much credence in anonymous tips."

"Not generally, no. But sometimes, like in this instance, turns out the tip is genuine."

"Anyone could have placed the earring there."

"Even you, according to Mr. Mason."

Henrietta gave a disbelieving laugh. "Do you know how ridiculous that sounds? To suggest Braydon thinks I killed the young woman and planted the other earring on him to throw suspicion?"

"I wouldn't say for sure he thinks that, miss. I'm just showing you how things look from this side of the law. A man has to examine every angle."

"You tole me you'd bring the bauble right back. Philips would never notice it missing, you said." Sheriff Yates stared at Hawkes as if he had suddenly grown two heads.

"I led Philips right to it," Hawkes said. "Practically tied it up with a bow."

"But what am I supposed to tell him?" Yates whined.

"You worry too much," Hawkes said. "He'll give you the ear-bob to put in the safe with the other one."

"But the other one's not there!" Yates's voice rose in exasperation.

"No one knows that except you," Hawkes said, in placating tones. "Philips doesn't have a key, does he?"

"No." Yates sounded calmer now.

"If the time comes, and I don't see it happening, that Philips demands both ear-bobs, you just play dumb. Like one must have got mislaid. Play it smart and you can even blame Philips. Claim he never gave you the second piece. After all, it'll be your word against his."

"I wish I'd never listened to you," Yates muttered as he prepared to take his leave.

"What did you just say?" Hawkes barked.

"Nuthin'."

As soon as he left, Hawkes opened the bottom drawer of his desk and pulled out his strong box. He unlocked it and scooped out a single ruby earring. Shame the little gal hadn't been wearing these when he killed her, but it was a worthwhile trophy nonetheless.

"Don't take your frustration out on me," Percy said as Henrietta slammed about the house.

"Everything about this town is frustrating," Henrietta said. "Can we just hurry up and find the pearls so we can put this trip behind us?"

"I've never seen you so anxious to move on before now. What's changed?"

Henrietta blew out a breath. "Everything. Nothing. I'm going out to camp. I'll meet you there."

Of course, going out to camp meant riding past the Copper Moon ranch house, and onto ranch land. *Not* that she was hoping to run into Braydon. But she thought he might have had the decency to tell her about the second earring.

Tell her what?

That the sheriff had found it among his things and he didn't know how it got there?

Which would solve exactly nothing.

But maybe they could talk.

Ha! Talking to Braydon is what had gotten her into this mess in the first place.

She felt much calmer by the time she reached camp.

A calm that was soon shattered by Braydon's arrival.

"What do you want?"

He dismounted in that easy way he had, loose-limbed, but purposeful. She hated the way her senses leapt to attention, as if every nerve-ending rose to just below the surface, attuned to his presence.

"Nice to see you, too." He didn't seem put off by her lack of warmth. If anything, he seemed to be enjoying it a little too much.

How could she be both drawn to him and despise him at the same time? She didn't trust him one grain. If Marshal Philips was indeed snooping around, convinced one or the other of them killed Paula Quinn, waiting for one of them to do something stupid and reveal their true killer nature ... Well, why wouldn't Braydon want it to be her who got fingered and not him?

"Miss me, Hen?" He stood so close she could see herself reflected in his eyes. She heaved out a breath. She didn't have it in her to lie.

She also didn't have it in her to step away when he reached to touch her, to trace her features with one callused fingertip.

"'Cause I sure as heck missed you." He gave her a crooked half smile. "Had Amanda and Laura both begging me to make up with you."

Don't fall for that famous Braydon Mason charm.

Her chin jutted up. "I don't believe you."

"You can ask them yourself next time we're at the ranch. Because I have an idea. Something to beat Hawkes at his own game. But I need your help."

She crossed her arms over her chest. "I'm listening."

"Hawkes is nothing if not greedy. If you can convince

him you and Percy found the pearls, he'll do anything to get his hands on them."

"And just how do you propose I do that?"

"With these, for starters."

She reached out and took the half dozen pearls Braydon held toward her in the palm of his hand. "These aren't even black pearls."

"You think Hawkes knows one pearl from the next? He'll believe you if you tell him that's the color they go after being buried all these years."

"Where did you get these?"

"From Zara. She wants them back, by the way."

"Let me guess. You want me to take these to Hawkes. Tell him Percy and I made our find, and we're packing up. But he's not getting cut in until I get my grandmother's earrings back."

"Right. Tell him the marshal is returning the one from the murder scene and you want the other one."

"Doesn't the marshal have both of them?"

"I don't believe that he does."

"Would you care to explain?"

"I think the marshal placed the one they found on Paula in the sheriff's safe. I think that Sheriff Yates, in cahoots with Hawkes, took it when marshal wasn't around and planted it in my bag. Then made up that story about the anonymous tip."

"You're saying, if Hawkes stole my earrings and killed Paula, placing one of them on the body, it stands to reason he still has the other earring."

"One thing I know. The man covets his kill trophies."

She studied Braydon closely, trying to gauge if he might have an ulterior motive. Even though he hadn't known his sister, it stood to reason he wanted to see her killer brought to justice. Particularly if that killer turned out to be Hawkes.

Plus, she absolutely wanted her earrings back.

"What if he denies having the other earring?"

"I think once he believes you and Percy found the pearl ship, he'll do anything to get his greedy hands on the pearls."

Henrietta wasn't sure if Braydon was worried about her facing Hawkes alone, or if he didn't fully trust her. At any rate, he insisted on accompanying her to Hawkes's spread and waiting out of sight a short distance down the driveway.

"You remember what you're going to say?" he asked her, for the dozenth time that morning.

"No," she drawled sarcastically. "I'm far too addle-brained to hold a simple thought in my head longer than a minute."

Braydon pursed his lips. "I swear, Henny, one of these days ..."

"One of these days, what?"

"One of these days you're going to open your mouth and be sorry about what comes out."

And one of these days I'll no longer be here, she thought. She'd miss their sparring matches. She'd also miss the way he looked at her when he thought she wasn't watching. Kind of like he was a match and she was the paper, and one simple brush against each other could cause instant combustion.

She sighed and tugged on the reins, guiding her horse toward the front of the house. Braydon had hurt her once. She wasn't about to let him close enough to do it again.

"Is Mr. Hawkes at home?" she asked the sad-eyed Mexican man who answered the door. No matter how badly she heard Hawkes treated his help, he seemed to have a steady supply of new ones to replace those who got fed up and moved on.

"You wait," the man said, in accented English after admitting her into the front hall.

Henrietta didn't have long to wait before she heard Hawkes's heavy tread coming down the tiled hallway toward her.

It was early in the day, but she could smell whiskey even before he got within arm's length. His gaze raked over her in a way that made her long for a bath immediately.

"Well, well, missy. Our little treasure hunter pays a visit. To what do I owe such a pleasure?"

"I'll be brief," she said.

"I like a woman who gets straight to the point."

"You have something that belongs to me. I'm in a position to make you a generous trade for the return of my property."

"Hell, sweetness." He moved in close enough she could see the bloodshot whites of his eyes as she tried to hold her breath against the whiskey fumes that seemed to be coming off his skin and his clothes as well as his breath. "I don't know what you think I have that's yours, but I feel mighty certain you have something I'd be interested in."

She tried not to flinch at his leering look as she took a step back and dug in her reticule. She pulled out the pearls, knotted in a silk handkerchief. She moved to a hall table, where she set down the handkerchief and untied the knot to reveal its contents.

"Percy and I have located Juan de Itrube's ship."

"You don't say!" He reached past her and grabbed up several of the pearls, clamping them between his meaty fingers. "You sure about that?"

"We found the ship's mast, so we kept digging. This is only a small sample of the pearls we found so far."

"I'll be." He licked his lips, leaving a glob of spittle in one corner.

"I'm prepared to make you a generous offer in exchange for my grandmother's ruby earring."

"I know nothing about—"

She brushed aside his denial. "You and I are business-people, Mr. Hawkes. The marshal has already returned the earring found at the murder scene. I require its mate, which I fully believe you have. I don't care about the particulars, how you happened to have them in the first place, or how one wound up in the hand of a dead girl."

He gave her a cunning look like that of a rabid animal. "Say I don't have it. But I know where it is and I can get it to you."

She gave him an assessing glance. "Bring the earring to the dig site tomorrow. I will exchange it for a generous measure of our cache. Meanwhile, do satisfy my curiosity. When did you remove the earrings from my home? And why did you plant one in the hand of your victim? Were you hoping to incriminate me in her murder?"

His mouth snapped shut in displeasure. "You ask too many questions."

"I have discovered it's the only way to discover the truth. Or the treasure."

His eyes narrowed into slits. "Nothing good ever came of asking too many questions."

CHAPTER 12

Braydon heaved a sigh of relief as he watched Henrietta come out the front door of Hawkes's place and mount her horse. He'd been more worried than he'd care to admit about sending her in there alone, but he hadn't seen any other way. Hawkes would have clammed up tight if he knew Braydon was involved.

He admired Henrietta's horsemanship as she rode toward him. *Who was he kidding?* He admired a whole lot more than the way she sat a horse. She had to be the most fascinating and capable woman he had ever met. He had faith that she could handle that vermin.

And if too much time had passed, he would have busted in there with both barrels blazing.

"What did he say?" he asked, as she rode up to where he waited on his mount.

"Claims he doesn't have it. But that he can get it. I told him to bring it out to the camp tomorrow."

"I don't like that," Braydon said. "You know he won't come alone."

Henrietta touched her heels to the flanks of her horse

and urged the mount to a canter, which he matched on his own horse. "And neither will you. If I can't goad him into a confession, maybe you can."

Clearly, she noticed his disapproving scowl. "What's your problem? I did what you asked."

Braydon shook his head. "Hawkes is up to something. I can feel it." He glanced her way. "Same as you, Henrietta. I can sense it when people lie to me. And I don't like it."

If he didn't know better, he might have been fooled by her innocent look. "I don't lie."

"I know you were seen talking to Paula Quinn a few days before she was killed."

"I didn't lie about it," she pointed out with maddening logic. "You never asked. I never said."

Exasperating woman!

"I'm asking now. What were you and Paula talking about?"

"Nothing to do with you, if that's what you were thinking. I didn't even know who she was at first. I only went out to see your mother's grave."

Braydon sawed on the reins so hard, his horse came to an abrupt halt and he almost flew over the front of his saddle. "You did what?"

Henrietta slowed and circled back to him. "I know it was pointless. I knew it at the time, but somehow, there I was anyway. Talking to a dead woman about her son. Hoping she might talk back and help me understand him better."

Braydon couldn't have been more shocked if she had clipped him on the jaw with her fist. "I only found out about her grave myself the other day."

"You said enough that I knew it was significant." She glanced down at the ground as if avoiding his gaze. "After you left, I found a piece of paper you must have dropped."

Henrietta glanced up, her expression unreadable. "It had her name and gravesite. I don't know why I went. I don't even know why I cared enough to try to learn more about what makes you tick." She shrugged. "Anyway, Paula must have wondered why some strange woman was muttering over her mother's head stone. I made up some lame excuse about being related to a Quinn family from Argentina, with whom I lost touch after they moved. We talked a bit. Decided we were not long-lost relatives and walked together until I turned off for Bullet. She was a lovely young woman. Full of curiosity about the world outside of Yuma." Henrietta gave a half laugh. "I'm afraid I made my life sound far more glamorous than it is. And not half so lonely."

Braydon felt his heart give a ridiculous hiccup. He'd never thought of Henrietta as lonely. To him, she was strong and independent, and far too self-sufficient to have time in her life to be lonely. Could that persona just be a mask she showed the rest of world?

"It's ironic, really. You know more about my sister than I do. Certainly, you spent more time with her."

"Which is one reason I agreed to help you wring a confession out of Hawkes, if he's the one responsible."

"I'll beat one out of him if that's what it takes," Braydon said. But he was still reflecting on Henrietta's words. He knew all too well how it felt to be surrounded by people and still feel lonely.

∼

HENRIETTA AND BRAYDON went their separate ways when they reached her place. Inside, she found a morose Percy hunched over a mound of crumpled papers spilling from the table onto the floor.

Lying on the floor next to his chair, broken into shards, was the piece from the ship's mast they'd retrieved from their dig.

Percy looked up at her entrance and eyed her with bleary, bloodshot eyes. He gave them a tired rub with the heels of his hands. "It's no use, Hen."

"What's no use?" She took a seat next to him, and laid a comforting hand on the back of his neck.

"It's not de 'Itrube's ship."

"Are you sure?"

"Beyond sure. This mast is part of one designed less than a hundred years ago. No way it could be from our lost pearl ship."

"Are we giving up then?"

"I'm afraid so. I don't doubt the ship's here some place. But I must have worked out the coordinates wrong. And I fear I've lost heart in the project."

Henrietta wasn't surprised to hear him say that. As long as she'd known Percy, he thrived on the fresh excitement of a new project. As time passed and the trail grew cold or boring, he was wont to abandon the current hunt for greener pastures. She'd recognized, when he chose to be here in town rather than out at camp, that his attention and enthusiasm were lagging.

"You know you have no follow-through," she told him good-naturedly as she rose.

"Where are you going?"

"I'm going to get changed. Then I'm going out to camp and start packing up. You should stay here and clean up this disaster." She waved a hand at the scattered evidence of Percy's makeshift science lab. "Amanda would have a fit if she saw what we've done to her mother's house."

"I'll have it put to rights before we leave," Percy said.

Leave.

The word rang hollowly in her ears. Normally, she was as excited as Percy to move onto their next adventure. This time felt different. This town felt different. There were people here she cared about. She'd miss Laura and Amanda, the closest thing she had to real girlfriends.

She wouldn't be here when Laura had her baby. Or see how Amanda fared with her dance hall project. Or find out which Mason brother got married next.

If it turned out to be Braydon ... The thought was too painful to contemplate further.

Out at the base camp, she pushed all thoughts of Braydon from her mind as she commenced the laborious job of collapsing the cots and folding the bedding and bug nets before she trucked them over to the wagon she'd driven out. Their tools, along with the tent, she'd come back for tomorrow. The tent was cumbersome to dismantle and she needed Percy's help with it.

She was so intent on what she was doing, she failed to hear the sound of riders approaching until it was too late. Belatedly, she whirled to face the intruders, aware her rifle was out of reach.

"Going somewhere, girlie?"

It was Hawkes, and he wasn't alone. He was accompanied by the same rag-tag group that had accosted her and Percy on the road near the ranch. The fat one was looking at her in a way that promised he had no intention of leaving her behind a second time.

She kept her voice casual. "I thought we agreed to meet tomorrow."

"You said that. I agreed to no such thing."

She waved a hand. "As you can see, now that we've

found the pearls, we're packing up to leave. Since you're here, would you mind giving me a hand with this tent?"

"What?" Hawkes's jaw dropped.

"You heard me. I can't dismantle the tent by myself."

Maybe she could somehow manage to have the tent collapse on him. Get to her rifle before—

Before what? There were four others besides him. Hardly favorable odds.

"I didn't come out here to be nobody's lackey," Hawkes said.

"Did you bring my earring?"

"Depends. Where's the pearls at?"

"Oh, no." She shook her head. "I'm nobody's fool. You get your pearls once I have my earring. And not before."

"See now, that's where you're sadly mistaken. The boys and I didn't come out here for *some* of them pearls. We came to get us the whole kit and kaboodle. Ain't that right, boys?" He looked to the other four as if for confirmation.

That's when Henrietta made her move. She dove for cover behind the tabletop, which was leaning up against a straight-backed chair. It was solid wood, better cover than anything else nearby. She reached into her boot and pulled out her pearl-handled revolver.

"You're not much of a partner, Hawkes. I told you, my earring for a percentage of the haul."

She peered around the edge of the table and saw Hawkes motioning the others with his rifle. "Get out there and find them pearls. I'll deal with the girl."

"Aw, boss, let me. I got an itch for her," leered the fat one.

Hawkes shot the fellow right where he sat in his saddle. The man's horse spooked and bolted, the injured rider clinging for dear life. Nearby, the horses hitched to her wagon shifted uneasily, but were too well-trained to bolt.

Hawkes addressed the remaining three, who sat staring at him, open-mouthed. "Anyone else feel like questioning my orders?" When no one responded, he said, "Good. What are you waiting for? Get out there and find them pearls."

The three men scattered. Which left Henrietta alone with Hawkes. Much better odds, particularly considering he didn't know she was armed.

"You can make this easy on everyone, Hawkes. Give me what I want, and I'll get you what you're after."

"You and your fancy man ought to be more careful," he cackled. "Waltzed right in the front door that day. You and him were out in the barn. Had me a lot of time to look around. Not much to see till I found your shiny baubles out in the open, just waiting for me."

Henrietta pressed her lips together in distaste at the thought of Hawkes snooping through the house, touching her things. She was trying to figure out how to circle around behind him without him seeing her when, out of the corner of her eye, she saw Braydon approaching on foot from one side, just out of Hawkes's range of vision. He wasn't alone, either. Brody was coming in from the other side.

She didn't know if she ought to be happy to see them or miffed they didn't think her capable of handling this on her own. At any rate, she did her best to keep Hawkes talking and distracted.

"I'd appreciate my jewelry back," she said. "You accomplished what you wanted. Marshal Philips found the earring in Braydon's saddlebag. No one's considering you a suspect in that girl's death."

"That's only one Mason out of the way when he goes down," Hawkes sneered. "Still leaves me six more to destroy."

"Why do you want the Copper Moon so bad?" Henrietta asked. "It's kind of run-down and in the middle of nowhere."

"Whole bunch of reasons that don't concern you. Why don't you come out from behind there and we can have ourselves a proper chat like we did earlier?"

"Not until I get my earring," Henrietta said. "You have to give me some reason to trust you." She darted a quick look over her shoulder, but there was no sign of the three buffoons. They were most likely down at the dig site. Let them dig to China. They still wouldn't find any pearls.

Meanwhile, Brody and Braydon were silently advancing on Hawkes.

"Throw your gun down, Hawkes. We have you surrounded!"

"Bloody hell!" Hawkes spurred his horse and it reared with a protest, hooves coming down frighteningly close to Braydon before Hawkes turned sharp and wheeled away, letting off a few wild shots as he did so.

Henrietta came out from behind her barricade slowly, her pistol still gripped tight. "There were others," she said. "Three of them."

"Taken care of," Brody said. "The twins will be dropping them with the marshal. I'm guessing those are the ones who assaulted you and Percy?"

She nodded. Leaning down, she tucked her pistol back inside her boot.

Braydon glanced around. "Looks like you're fixing to leave."

"That's right. Percy has confirmed we're not in the right spot. He's already excited about our next project."

"Does that mean no pearls?" Braydon asked.

"Only these." Henrietta passed him the pearls he'd given

her as bait to trap Hawkes. "And no ruby earring," she said sadly.

"Don't be so quick about that," Braydon said as he dug through his vest pocket. "I don't want anyone getting the wrong idea or anything. Kind of helped myself to this out at Hawkes's earlier today. After you and him had your little chat, I went back and waited till he left."

He reached for Henrietta's hand and laid the earring in her palm, closing her fingers over it to keep it safe. Her skin prickled and grew warm from his touch.

"You were convinced he had it all along."

"Not too hard to anticipate his moves after all these years."

"You knew he'd come out here tonight after the pearls, not wait to meet me tomorrow."

"Stood to reason," he said, his gaze looking straight through her and melting her insides to the core.

She turned to Brody in an effort to distract herself. "Rest assured, you'll never know we were here. Percy and I appreciated that you trusted us enough to stay here and go after the treasure."

"Happy to oblige," Brody said. "Just sorry to hear you came up empty-handed." He cleared his throat. "I know Laura and Amanda will be sorry to hear of you leaving. I wager everyone here will miss you when you're gone."

She nodded. "I'll miss them too." What was wrong with her? She'd never felt sad before at the prospect of packing up and moving on.

ALL TOLD, it took another four days to clear up their base camp and put things back the way they'd been, including the dig site and Amanda's house. There was also time needed with the marshal. Henrietta shared his frustration at the lack of a breakthrough in the murder, but she also knew Hawkes was slippery. She could only pray one of these days he'd make a move that would see him brought to justice.

"Keep in touch, Miss Henrietta. Right now, we have your earring as evidence from the crime scene, but I'll do my best to see it back to you as quickly as possible."

"Don't you have them both?" she asked innocently. "One from the crime scene and one that you found on Braydon?"

He harrumphed uncomfortably. "It appears that unknown parties planted false evidence on Mr. Mason. He was never truly a suspect."

"And the other earring?"

"Don't rightly know what to tell you, Miss." He paused. "Now that I think about it, why don't you stop by the office on your way out of town? I do believe we've hung onto your property long enough. I'd hate for something to happen to the other piece. Funny the way things like that tend to happen around here. Evidence disappearing and reappearing and the like. Very shoddy practices."

"I'll be sure and do that."

WITH THEIR BELONGINGS safely packed away in steamer trunks aboard the wagon, Percy and Amanda drove to the stagecoach depot in Bullet. Once there, the driver took one look at their things and flat-out refused to take them to Yuma.

"But you brought us both out here, sir," Percy recalled. "Even if it was on different trips. You were well compensated for the service."

The driver shook his head stubbornly. "New policy. One trunk per passenger."

Percy threw his hands in the air. "I will be sorely relieved to leave this backwater town behind and get back to London, where things are civilized."

Henrietta said nothing.

"Don't you agree, Hen?"

"Hmmmm. What?" She was busy looking around at all that was familiar. Georgina's café. Storm's mobile library. The schoolhouse where Laura used to teach. The pretty park that backed down to the river. She could almost envision Amanda's music hall on the empty lot at the end of the street.

"I'm at a loss," Percy said. "We haven't much time to get to Yuma to catch our train. We can't drive there in the wagon, because we have no way to get the horse and wagon back here to the livery."

"Right," Henrietta said, giving herself a mental shake.

Just then, a familiar rig came charging down the street toward them, Amanda at the reins with Laura at her side, literally hanging on to her hat.

"Thank goodness!" Laura exclaimed as Amanda drew the rig to a halt. Amanda leapt out first. "You never came to say goodbye," she chided Henrietta. "We were so afraid we might miss you."

Henrietta swallowed thickly. "I'm not very good at good-byes," she admitted. In truth, saying goodbye was something she avoided every time she moved on, starting with her defection from Argentina and her family.

"Fine then," Laura said, as she hugged her. "Until we meet again."

Henrietta sighed. If only she believed that might happen.

Held tight in Laura's hug, she couldn't help peering over her friend's shoulder, on the lookout for a certain dark-haired man astride his mount, but the street remained mockingly empty. It would appear, as far as Braydon was concerned, she was already out of sight, out of mind.

"I say," Percy said. "I don't suppose there's a chance you two lovely ladies could accompany us to Yuma, then return here with the wagon and horses?"

Amanda and Laura looked at each other. "We could do that, couldn't we?" They both nodded in agreement.

"Right, then," Percy said. "We need to get a move on. We've got a train to catch."

Laura laid a hand atop his forearm. "Sorry to hold things up, but I'm afraid I'm in need of ..." She flushed prettily. "I'll just pop over to the café. I shan't be long."

"I'll come with you," Amanda said.

Several minutes passed, then several minutes more. Percy consulted his pocket watch and sighed loudly with each passing minute. "What on heavenly earth could be taking them so long?"

Henrietta slanted him a look. "You want to question a lady in the family way about her visit to the 'necessary'?"

He blushed to the roots of his hair. "Of course not."

"They're doing us a big favor," Henrietta added. She was thrilled the ladies had come to see them off, even if their presence made leaving all the more difficult.

Finally, Percy gave her a push in the direction of the café. "Go then, Hen. See if you can find out what's holding them up."

She crossed Main Street carefully, even though there was little traffic. How could she have thought Bullet squat and ugly? It was a pretty little town, neatly kept, with residents who cared about their surroundings. Like Georgina, and the pretty window boxes beneath the windows of the café.

"Henrietta!" Georgina greeted her. "How lovely of you to stop in. I was afraid you might just ride out of town without a backward glance. I'm glad I was mistaken. We'll miss you around these parts."

Henrietta huffed out a breath. If one more person told her they'd miss her ... She glanced around. "Have you seen Laura and Amanda? They were headed this way."

"They were just here," Georgina said. "Heard them say they were popping over to see Storm for a minute."

"Pop over where?" she asked in exasperation.

"The park. Down by the river." Georgina caught Henrietta's hand in hers. "I heard you weren't much of one for good-byes."

Henrietta swallowed thickly. This was getting to be the longest, most drawn-out goodbye in history. After giving Georgina a quick hug, the image of Percy, pacing and scowling, set her off at a near run. She knew the park. It was a popular spot with the townsfolk because it was close enough to the river for easy irrigation. The perennially grassy surface was perfect for family picnics and ballgames and afforded a safe place for little ones to run around.

Her steps slowed. Georgina must have been mistaken. Her friends were nowhere to be seen.

She turned away but not before she caught a glimpse of movement near the charming white gazebo, which held a place of prominence in the middle of the park.

She redirected her gaze. Her movements froze as Braydon stepped from the shadows of the gazebo into the sunlight. Slowly he descended the half dozen steps that led to the grass. A dozen long strides brought him to her side.

Her heart pounded so loudly, the blood roared in her ears and made it impossible to hear a thing.

She didn't need sound. Braydon's expression said it all. His eyes were warm on hers, melting her insides into a mushy mess.

"This was planned," she said.

"Percy warned me you weren't one for goodbyes. I figured you'd bolt if I said anything sooner. I thought I'd let you take a good, long look at what you were leaving behind. Let you figure it out yourself, if you really want to go or not."

She tilted her chin. "I was half-expecting you to try and talk me into staying."

"I figured as much," Braydon said. "Had your arguments all prepared too, I wager."

"You got me," she said, biting back a half smile.

He reached for her hand and held it lightly in his, light enough that she could easily pull away. "Do I, Henny? Do I really have you?"

She gazed up at him, this man who knew her so well. Maybe even better than she knew herself. If she stayed, the life they created together would be anything but dull. They would always be trying to outthink and outsmart and outmaneuver each other. Which ought to keep life really interesting. Even in a small town like Bullet.

A town where she had friends. A town where she would be part of a big, rowdy family. On her terms, this time.

"I grew up with nine brothers, you know."

"Which is about the same number of mothers I had growing up."

"Is that why I understand you and you understand me?"

"I think that's only one of the reasons. Most of all, I think I understand you because I love you."

It was all she needed to hear. Everything she needed to hear. She launched herself toward him.

He caught her easily. "Does this mean you'll stay?"

"Forever and ever." She wound her arms around his neck and pulled his head down close. Their mouths met and mated with a fevered ecstasy that stole her breath and pushed all else from her mind, save the rightness of being in his arms.

His hands slid down and cupped her derriere in a possessive fashion, his palms warming her skin through the fabric of her men's-style pants. "Did I ever tell you I like the way these hug your butt?"

Henrietta grabbed his ass and squeezed hard. "Did I ever tell you I like the way these hug yours?"

Braydon threw back his head and laughed. "We are going to have so much fun!"

THE PARK'S gazebo was decked in yards and yards of ribbon, shiny white posts adorned with sprays of wild flowers. Rows of benches next to chairs borrowed from the café offered guests a spot to sit. The tent from Percy and Henrietta's base camp had been set up to shelter folks who found the sunlight too intense.

Smack in the center of the gazebo, the seven Mason brothers formed a straight line as they waited. All eyes were on Henrietta, on Percy's arm, as the pair wound their way across the grass, and through the guests to the gazebo stairs.

Henrietta was stunning in an antique satin gown that had been worn by her grandmother and shipped to Bullet from England. In her ears, the ruby earrings winked in the sunlight. She and Percy followed her attendants up the gazebo steps.

"Who gives this woman to be joined in holy matrimony, to this man?" the reverend intoned.

"I do." With a quick kiss, Percy released Henrietta to take her place alongside Braydon.

From where she stood next to Amanda, Storm, one of the bridesmaids, snuck a subtle glance at Blake Mason, flanked by his brothers. She knew Blake's big secret.

It was nothing compared with the secret she carried with her every day. A secret that haunted her dreams and made all hope for the future impossible.

Thanks for reading *Braydon's Bride*. You might not know how important reader reviews are, but they mean a lot. Just a short sentence saying you enjoyed the book goes a long way with new readers and puts a smile on this author's face.

Review wherever your purchased *Braydon's Bride* or on Goodreads or BookBub .

And please keep in touch

Website: KathleenLawless.com
Facebook: facebook.com/kathleenlawlessnovels
Instagram: instagram.com/kathleenflawless
TikTok: tiktok.com/@kathleenflawless

If you haven't already done so, sign up for my VIP Reader's Newsletter and be the first to hear about free books, fan-priced sales, and my new series. http://eepurl.com/bVosbI

Keep reading for a preview of Seven Brides for Seven Brothers, book 4, *Blake's Bride*.

Dear Reader

The American West in the last half of the nineteenth century offers my heroines a chance to assert their independence and also introduce them to a hero who is their match in every way. My characters have their own ideas of right and wrong, good versus evil, and deal with it on their terms. It wasn't called the Wild West for nothing. Life was about conquest, survival and persistence,

I love writing a historical genre where the reader, by the simple act of picking up the book, instantly suspends disbelief. She easily forgets about her world and her woes in a tale where no one needs to empty the dishwasher or take out the trash, and adventure lies around every corner.

As an author, it's fun to carry her away to a time and place where anything could, and often did, happen. The customs of the day and the manner of dress might be different from today's world, but people are still people. They laugh, love, hurt and heal. Celebrate and mourn. They live life large. And in the untamed wildness of the settling of the west anything can happen.

Turn the page to read an excerpt from Book 4, *Blake's Bride*.

BLAKE'S BRIDE - EXCERPT

It was a perfect day for a wedding. The gazebo in the town's park was decked in yards and yards of ribbon, shiny white posts adorned with sprays of wild flowers. Smack in the center of the gazebo, the seven Mason brothers waited in a straight line.

Storm, alongside her fellow bridesmaid Amanda, wiped her sweaty palm on the skirt of her frock and clutched her nosegay tightly. This was her first time being a bridesmaid. It was also her first time in such a fancy dress, edged in lace and all, crafted by her own hand.

From her vantage point, Storm watched Henrietta the bride, appear on the arm of her long-time friend, Percival Bloom.

As the ceremony got underway, Storm snuck a subtle glance at Blake Mason, flanked by his brothers. From Laura Mason, the first bride, she had learned Blake had a secret, something she could relate to. She had a few of her own. If only her 'big secret' was as innocent as Blake's. Lots of folks out west couldn't read. As a librarian, she was no stranger to witnessing their struggles, and happy when she was able to help.

After the ceremony, she saw Laura beckoning to her. "Did you have a chance to talk to Blake, yet?" Laura lowered her voice so no one near them could hear what she was saying.

"Not yet." Already, Storm was regretting her offer to try to help Blake learn to read. She had only met a few folks in her travels who were word-blind, and eventually managed to overcome the affliction to learn to read simple words.

"Well, there he is, all alone over there." Laura gave her a tiny push. "Now's your chance."

Head high, Storm nodded. It was important she maintain control, in every aspect of her life. Especially where men were concerned.

"Laura said I should come ask you to dance," she said brightly.

Poor Blake reminded her of a trapped animal, eyes sliding from side to side as if seeking escape.

"Weddings make me uncomfortable too," she confided. "You, at least, have had some practice lately, what with three of your brothers tying the knot in the last short while. Do you boys really build a new cabin for each couple on the ranch?"

"Yes, ma'am." Blake swallowed thickly, his Adam's apple bobbing with the movement. "I'm afraid I'm not much on the dance floor, Miss Storm."

"Good." She took his arm. "Neither am I. Two left feet, I believe, is the expression."

She schooled herself not to freeze up or flinch when she felt his hand rest tentatively on her waist. Not every touch was designed to inflict pain. She found a slight modicum of comforting in knowing he was at least as uncomfortable as she was.

Get your copy of *Blake's Bride* today or keep reading to see more books by Kathleen.

Mail Order Noelle

Chelsea's Choice

Lila: Rescue Me Mail Order Brides

Here Come the Brides Volume 1

Here Come the Brides Volume 2

Sweet Contemporary Romance

Frannie (Always a Bridesmaid)

Baxter (Last Man Standing)

Blue Sky Island

One Cinderella Spring

One Stolen Summer

One Fantasy Fall

One Wondrous Winter

Sweet Christmas Romance Novellas

Holly's Wish

No Groom at the Inn

Steamy Contemporary Romance
SECRET SEDUCTIONS

Her Untamed Cowboy - Book 1

Her Undercover Cowboy - Book 2

Her Unwilling Cowboy - Book 3

Who Needs a Cowboy! - Book 4

Intimate Strangers

Steamy Historical Romance

Taboo

Unmasked

Reckless Rogues - Box Set of the 2 Books

Romantic Suspense

Final Heat

Afterburn

Women's Fiction

Fabulous at Fifty

For a complete book list visit KathleenLawless.com

To be the first to hear about Kathleen's new releases, special fan pricing sales, and also receive a free book, sign up for her VIP Reader Newsletter at http://eepurl.com/bVosbI

ABOUT THE AUTHOR

USA Today Bestselling Author, Kathleen Lawless, blames a misspent youth watching Rawhide, Maverick and Bonanza for her fascination with cowboys, which doesn't stop her from creating a wide variety of interests and occupations for her many alpha male heroes.

With nearly 50 published novels to her credit, she enjoys pushing the boundaries of traditional romance into historical romance, contemporary romance, romantic suspense and women's fiction.

She makes her home in the Pacific Northwest and loves to hear from her readers.

Sign up for Kathleen's VIP Reader Newsletter to receive updates, special giveaways and fan-priced offers. http://eepurl.com/bVosbı

KathleenLawless.com
Goodreads | BookBub
Facebook | Instagram | TikTok

amazon.com/Kathleen-Lawless/e/B001IXS2SA

goodreads.com/kathleenlawless

bookbub.com/authors/kathleen-lawless

facebook.com/kathleenlawlessnovels

instagram.com/kathleenflawless

tiktok.com/@kathleenflawless